THE RISE

OF

ONYX

Angelina Singer

Dedicated with love to my grandfather, John B. Calcagno, "Nono", who has been my biggest encourager and always tells me to never stop. I don't plan to anytime soon, Nono. And it's all thanks to you.

VOLUME ONE: THE MACHINE

CHAPTER 1

Luna's calm footfalls fill the acoustics of the Grand Hall, where Onyx has been charged with the responsibility of producing enough orbs to keep the entire human population from dying out. She approaches him, smiling, despite his extreme boredom and feelings of utter despondency.

"Hello, Onyx."

He lifts his head up from where it was resting on the back of the throne, and looks down at her with weary, eyes not unlike a cloudy blue sky.

"Hello, Luna."

She walks a bit closer to him, just reveling in his presence even though she must stay far away from the current that runs through him now. A silence loaded with desperation fills the space between them, as the human portions of their hybrid forms become desperate for each other.

"How is… everything here going?" She motions to the area around the throne, but Onyx understands that she means everything in the Sorting Room, as well as the orb production.

"Just fine, I think. I'm new at this, but I am also getting quite tired of it."

Luna tilts her head slightly. "You're tired? I thought you don't get tired anymore, because of the current? At least, that's what Griffin told me."

Onyx shakes his head. "Well, I don't get physically tired anymore, perhaps that is what he meant. I just mean that sitting here, and not really doing anything, is quickly wearing on me."

Luna nods, and frowns sadly. "Well, it's important, what you're doing, you know. You saved all of us."

Onyx sighs. "I know, but I do wish I had the chance to make that choice on my own. I was volunteered to do this, and even though I didn't know what I was getting into and didn't really want to, there was not time to find a suitable replacement before the entire Upperworld was sucked into the portal."

"Well, I think you are amazing. I really do."

"That makes one of us."

Luna takes a step closer to the throne.

"Not too close Luna, I'm dangerous. Don't forget that. I could not live with myself if I...." He cannot even bring himself to finish that sentence, but he counters with another one instead. "No wonder Zephyr always seemed so cold. This is a miserable existence."

"Maybe it's worse for you because you are part humanoid."

Onyx nods. "It is possible. Although, I guess we'll never truly know about Zephyr's origin. Not that it matters now – he is long gone."

She hastily changes the subject before Onyx gets too upset again. "Well, Evander and Griffin are working to get you out of there, isn't that exciting! There is so much to be grateful for, Onyx. I'm grateful for this. I'm grateful for the chance to have you back, even though nothing is guaranteed."

Onyx brushes a piece of his short, shaggy, pale blonde hair out of his eyes. "You and me both, Luna. Any day now, I am trying to believe I'll be freed. But it is steadily getting harder and harder to fully believe that."

"I understand that, I do. But you have to stay positive, please? Can you do that, at least for me?" Luna is not accustomed to being the stronger one – as long as she has existed, it has always been Onyx to make her stronger and keep her safe. Now it is her turn to do the same for him, and she's not used to the responsibility it holds.

"I'm going to try, Luna. That's the best I can say about that right now. Beyond that, I really don't know." He runs his hand through his bleached-blonde hair and sighs again.

"Whatever happens, we'll at least be able to say we tried."

"That is true, but oh my pod I really do hope it works. I can't do this forever. I just can't."

✳✳✳

"Griffin, I have to attend to my shift in the record keeping office for a while. In the meantime, why don't you send me the digital plans you have for the machine, so we can get right on that?" Evander continues walking toward his office where much of the Upperworld's data is kept under heavy security. His protegé, Griffin, follows excitedly on his heels.

"Sure thing, Evander. I'm just happy we might get to help Onyx, I can tell he is starting to falter quite rapidly."

Evander slowly nods. "That is true, Onyx is merely a placeholder, nothing more. He was never cut out for that position of permanent stagnation - he's a worker, and needs to get up and do things more stimulating than just sitting in a chair."

"So, I'll keep working on it, and check back with you soon, I guess?"

Evander nods at Griffin as he closes the door of the record keeping office behind him. The young record keeper shows a lot of promise, but often lacks tact and can be a bit clingy at times. Luckily, Evander has patience to spare - if Griffin had anyone else assigned to him as a mentor, he may not have been so lucky in that department.

Griffin makes his way back to his pod where he has saved his experimental documents on his computer. The time machine, as he has begun to call his little pet project, is largely theoretical, but he is confident that bringing it to life could bring with it some fascinating capabilities for the Upperworld - perhaps it could even function as a sort of insurance clause to avoid fiascos like the one Luna got herself sucked into what feels like forever ago now. So much has happened since the day Delphine mixed up the orbs and Luna was sent to Earth in her place. But thankfully, things are better now and Luna

7

is safely back in the Upperworld where she belongs. Zephyr wanted her killed, but Onyx went down to earth to protect her from the assassin Zephyr sent after her. It had been a crazy time handling all of that as well as the revolution taking place in the Upperworld as Zephyr himself began dying on the job - and Onyx unwittingly took over the reigns. Now Griffin hopes to be instrumental in reinstating Onyx back as a mentor instead of just the very stagnant work of being The Most High Being. This was his chance to do something revolutionary - because bending time and space was no small matter, as he knows all too well.

His computer comes to life at the scan of his thumbprint on the touchscreen, and then he inputs his password to open his very experimental documents. He had been toying around with some digital blueprints as of late, purely for fun before he realized that this machine might actually have a very real purpose. Now, he looked at his work with freshly critical eyes, knowing that it would be responsible for the safety of real lives - both Onyx's life, as well as the brave souls who would agree to be the first time travelers in human history. A small bead of sweat emerges on his forehead as he takes a deep breath, breathing in both the potential for history to be made, and for the utter disaster that could occur if the machine somehow malfunctions, pod forbid.

CHAPTER 2

Luna drops yet another orb into its appropriate receptacle tube in the Sorting Room. The process has become so incredibly natural for her now - she doesn't even need to give it a second thought. Onyx had taught her well, but her natural ability did the rest. And right now, it is a blessing that she can carry out her very important job without much brain power being expelled - her mind is elsewhere at the moment.

I can't stop worrying about Onyx. I know Evander and Griffin are doing what they can to get him off of the throne, but it might not work. And then what happens to him? What happens... to us?

Her constant thoughts bounce around her head relentlessly as she tries to clear her mind and focus on her tasks at hand. Walking across the vast Sorting Room carrying an orb in the palm of her hand, Luna tries to focus on some sensory details to ground her in the moment she is in. In the past, this tactic had worked to steady her mind in moments of turmoil, but at the moment, her efforts seem fruitless.

After depositing the most recent orb into the receptacle, she pauses to catch her breath and steady herself once more, lest she make a fatal mistake - for real, this time.

So much has happened, and I never had time to process it all. Onyx is trapped. I'm here doing my job alone. And Jade... oh, poor, troubled Jade...

A single tear slides down her cheek as she remembers the truly horrific way Jade let her level of prestige go to her head, which resulted in her very untimely death. She was never that close to Jade, actually, perhaps a bit intimidated by her. But there's something in Luna's mind that keeps pushing her back to the moment she met Jade and the way things went so sour so fast. And amidst the memories of her former superior, her very graphic death in the throne room has branded itself with the hot iron of reality and its terrifying wiles.

"Hi, um, Luna?"

Luna composes herself long enough to turn around and meet the calm gaze of the ever-joyful Brielle. The younger sorter has started to look up to Luna, which, flattering as it is, adds even more pressure for Luna to be as perfect at her job as she can be.

"Oh, hello Brielle. Is there something specific I can do for you?"

"Me? How about you? You seem... more upset than usual."

Luna nods, realizing that keeping her guard up is a useless endeavor. "A lot has happened, yes. And I suppose I just now am processing it all."

Brielle nods and pats Luna's shoulder kindly, even though she doesn't have the capacity to experience or understand human emotions the way Luna does.

"I can only imagine what you must be feeling. Of course, I don't totally understand, but I can try. If you, ever want to talk about it." Brielle smiles sweetly, and brushes aside a bit of her freshly-tinted metallic golden hair. Luna thinks to herself how nicely the color suits her in context with Brielle's signature bright smile, but the words don't make it to her lips before she crumbles in a pile of tears.

"Alright Luna, maybe you should take a break? I'll let Sebastian know you need some time to make sense of everything."

Luna nods almost imperceptibly amidst the tears, and she fights the urge to laugh in between it all, since the reason she's crying is ambiguous even to herself. She knew that Sebastian, her shift manager, would understand and happily take over for her. But there is always that subtle sting living in the pit of her stomach that reminds her of her own inadequacy.

✳✳✳

Hard at work in his office, Griffin continues studying the blueprints of the time machine that he developed, and begins drafting a list of the supplies he'll need to bring it to life. A lot of the list is fairly self-explanatory, like welding tools and scrap metal to provide the protective frame for the wildly intricate technology beneath it. The more detailed structures to be at the heart of the machine involved some deep studies of physics, gravity, and wormholes - some of which is vastly theoretical, at best. Griffin fights the urge to scream at his monitor and give up, but he continues on. Finding loopholes in the laws of physics is exactly as difficult as it sounds, if not more.

Okay, it seems that the most important thing is to attach a power source to the flux capacitor, which should make time jumping possible.

He smiles to himself as the first part of his conundrum shows signs of defeat. As he prepares to make the fatal kill and triumph over it, he remembers some more logistics and quickly enters them into his computer.

We'll need a remote access point for the travelers - so they can come back from wherever, or whenever, they are. And also, we're lacking a power source. I'll have to talk to Evander about figuring out that part - I never can figure that part out.

Inventing gadgets is nothing new to Griffin, even if time travel is. He has notoriously become known in the Upperworld as the bona fide tech genius, similarly to Evander. Both of them had outfitted the recent revolution against Zephyr with a whole slew of soundproofing devices to keep meetings private, as well as conveniently located electronic nutrient dispensers in the main hall. Everyone who's anyone in the Upperworld knows that Griffin and Evander are the ones who could potentially pull this off.

Griffin sighs to himself, thinking about all the pressure this places on his still relatively-young shoulders.

I want to help Onyx, I really do. But this is so foreign and risky. Either I get this machine to work and we accomplish what we need to, or I don't and Onyx will just have to suffer. Or worse - maybe the machine works, but we irreparably change time and human history.

He tries his best to shake off that latest bout of irrational yet rational fears, and refocuses on the critically-important task at hand. That is, until he hears the restricted access door open behind him.

"Griffin, how's the time machine coming along?"

He spins around in his chair and sighs, while forcing a polite smile in Evander's direction.

"Oh you know, it's... coming. I've been playing around with a lot of different options, nothing is truly sitting right with me just yet."

"Can I take a look?"

Griffin nods dejectedly, happy to step away from his incredibly challenging work after hours of mentally draining focus. A small eternity seems to go by as Evander wordlessly clicks, moves, and rubs his chin at the digital images, graphs, and lists that Griffin has compiled.

"This looks... somewhat promising. I have some questions about some of the theories and accouterments that you have suggested."

"Of course, ask away."

Evander pauses to phrase his question as well as he can. "Without seeming immature in my asking, how are we sure this won't mess up anything irreparably?"

"That's the thing - we're not."

CHAPTER 3

"Well if you miss him so much, just go to the throne room and talk to him."

Luna smiles through the tears clouding her face while trying not to snap at the well-meant yet infuriating suggestion from Brielle.

"I would, and I probably will in a little while, but you don't understand... there's more to it than just that. He's not the same. He's not happy, doesn't feel good. And not being able to be close to him is *killing me*."

Brielle's eyes widen with concern at Luna's latest comment. "Wait, you mean you are actually dying? Let's get straight to the infirmary and -"

"No! I'm *fine*."

The finality of Luna's words slaps Brielle in the face, and she recoils with a note of confusion plastered on her face. Luna softens her approach in response.

"I just mean... I'm sorry, I didn't mean to, I mean, I'm okay, Brielle. But this is still really hard. On Earth, humanoids talk more figuratively than literally often times - it's just part of their speech patterns. I must have picked it up, I should have explained..."

Brielle shakes a few strands of her golden hair out of her face. "I understand... there are just a lot of things that I won't understand. And I'm working on being okay with that, somehow."

Luna smiles through her tears and gently grabs Brielle's hand. "I really do appreciate you being there for me when I needed you most. You're an amazing friend, you know."

"It was the proper thing to do. We must support each other for the Upperworld to subsist and thrive."

Luna smiles at Brielle's paraphrase of the Upperworld handbook database, but shakes her head almost imperceptibly. After all she has experienced on Earth, it is amazing to reflect on how far she has come, and how little she now relates to her Upperworld counterparts.

Earth changed me. Now I just hope that was a good thing, and not something I'll regret. Not that I really had a choice, anyway. Luna sighs, thinking about all that has happened and all that is to come.

"You know, Onyx really saved us all. At least, that's what Evander told me." Brielle pats her hand reassuringly, but she still fails to understand the complexity of Luna's emotions. But it's nothing personal, of course. She just wasn't born to be equipped for that kind of thing.

"Oh, believe me, I do know that. I just wish we had known he'd be stuck for a while until we figure out a solution."

"Would you have hesitated?"

"Hesitated to what?"

"Hesitated to let him go do what he needed to do?"

"Oh, I guess not. Seeing how it would be an automatic death sentence for everyone and the entire human race."

15

Brielle huffs in frustration. "Well, that's the *right* answer, I guess. But what do you feel about it? I don't really know anything about emotions, since I've never experienced them and never will, I guess. But I have a hunch that maybe you wouldn't have gone along with it so calmly had you known the outcome."

Luna's violet eyes blink away some lingering tears. "You know, I think you're right, Brielle. But I still don't want to admit that I would put everyone in jeopardy just to keep him near me."

Both sorters break eye contact to look around at the blank walls of Luna's pod, still beckoning for some more personalized decorations. She hasn't had a lot of free time lately, and decorating her space was never a priority, what with all the craziness that has been going on. Regardless of the lack of creativity on the walls, Luna feels more at home in her own pod than any place on Earth. At least, as at home as she can be when she's not in Onyx's arms. That home would have to wait.

"Brielle, not that I don't like having you here, but would you mind terribly if I go to see him now?"

"No, not at all! Yeah, let me just grab my stuff and..."

"Alone, please."

Brielle pauses and nods slowly, and then backs out of Luna's pod. The door shuts behind her as Luna runs her hand through her tangled, midnight tresses. After a few deep breathes and fixing her hair, she too leaves her pod and begins the long walk through the purplish fog of the

Upperworld toward the throne room where her beloved has been stationed indefinitely.

She keeps her breath as steady as she can throughout the long walk, even managing to smile at the familiar faces of the other sorters and record keepers as she goes. The walk itself seems to be two eternities long, and Luna hasn't been able to decide what's worse - not seeing him at all or seeing him suffer. Going to visit Onyx is becoming to feel like a rather selfish endeavor, as if seeing him helped her a bit but made the waiting time harder for him. At the moment though, Luna succumbs to her need to see him - she's half-human, after all.

✳✳✳

"So what do you think about the power source? Any ideas?"

Evander scratches his head in response to Griffin's query. As the in-house technology expert, he always feels obliged to know these kinds of things, but time-travel is so far out of his wheelhouse that he's at a loss about as much as everyone else. And Griffin has been showing signs of prodigy, so as much as it pained Evander to admit, Griffin might just have the upper hand in this matter.

"Well, it's going to have to be something that can withstand inter-dimensional travel with a robust docking system to link it both back to us here and the travelers. Speaking of which, who do you think would be the best person to send?"

Griffin blinks, wondering what Evander is getting at. "I honestly kind of thought it'd be one of us going…"

Evander stops in his tracks and turns around in the desk chair he's sitting in. "Excuse me?"

"Well, Luna certainly is not a good choice, as she's been through enough already and studies have shown that repeated molecular scrambling can be bad for your health if done too frequently."

Evander nods slowly. "That is true. But there are plenty of other sorters who may be able to."

"No one else understands all the ramifications of everything the way we do. Also, it's a pretty sensitive matter, so I doubt Onyx wants just anyone to go poking around in his past."

"That is… also true. So, what do you suppose we do?"

Griffin gulps slowly, wishing that the knot forming in his throat would dissolve faster than it seems to be. "Well, maybe we should just ask him? But it's probably going to end up being one of us."

Evander pauses, and deeply inhales the stale air of the office. "You make some excellent points, Griffin. I'm not thrilled with the idea of risking my life with something as experimental and theoretical as time travel, but I think I'd be willing to do it for my friend."

Griffin exhales, relieved that his mentor agrees with him regarding this matter of time travel. "Okay, that's good to hear. But I suppose we should wait until the machine is finalized - wouldn't want to get his hopes up in case we can't actually get it to work."

"That is also very true." Evander gets up from the computer chair and pats him on the back. "I'm very proud of you, Griffin. Your bravery and inventive spirit will take you very far in this life."

CHAPTER 4

From his vantage point on the throne, Onyx can see Luna approaching from the main entrance of the Grand Hall. The long hallway leads straight to him, and he revels in the fact that her slow, metered pacing takes as long as it does, as he loves seeing her in person. Also, the added motion her approach brings is a welcome respite from the bland environment lacking in any kind of visual interest. He sits up a little from his previously reclined posture, and can't fight even the tired smile spreading over his weary face.

"Hello, Onyx." Luna's small voice reverberates through the large room - the acoustics of the Grand Hall are, well, grand.

"Hello, Luna. How are things beyond these hallowed halls?" His query about the world outside the building he is imprisoned in serves as yet another reminder how dire his circumstance is.

"Fine, I suppose. It's hard, to be without you. But I'm okay, mostly." She smiles at him as she settles on the padded chair that Brielle had recently brought for her to sit on while visiting Onyx. "Your eyes... they're kind of... glowing."

Onyx nods. "I know, it's a side effect of the current. My hair is glowing a bit too. That's what Evander told me, anyway."

"Does it hurt?"

Onyx sighs. "No, the glowing is painless. Can't say the same about the rest of me though. No one ever tells you how painful it is to sit for so long."

Luna nods slowly, and then crosses her legs and leans back in her own chair at the base of the tall throne. Looking up at Onyx, she can feel his essence and life force floating around her, but it is practically treacherous to be unable to physically hold him the way she used to.

"But Evander and Griffin are on it. I trust that their theory will work and they'll get what they need to set me free from this pod-forsaken chair."

"Is it going to bother you, though?"

"Is what going to bother me?"

"Having Evander and Griffin go digging through your past?"

Onyx pauses to consider her question, and then opens his mouth before abruptly shutting it again. He rests his chin in the palm of his hand. When he finally does speak, the answer surprises her.

"No, not at all, really."

"Really?"

"Really. In fact, they're doing me an incredible favor. Without them, I literally would never get off this chair. They're giving me hope. They're giving *us* hope."

Luna nods. "Right, but, it's a little odd, still. I mean, they're going to see... your mother. Even you've never seen your mother."

"Well, that's not entirely true..."

Luna's jaw drops open. "Huh?"

"Yes, it's true." Onyx pauses to let her take it all in. "When I first found out about myself - and about you - I did a little digging. Deep in the record keeping files, Evander keeps tabs on everything. Of course, it required more clearance than he had, but being the amazing technological expert that he is, he hacked into it and let me see at least what she looked like. She even has my eyes."

"Wow, that is… incredible. How did you, feel about that?"

Onyx smiles to himself, with a bit of sadness pricking him at the edges of his mouth. "Well, I was mostly just intrigued. And a bit sad, of course. Given the circumstances. And then I was a bit angry, and well, you surely must understand…"

Luna nods. "That's the thing with you and I - we understand each other, better than anyone else, because we have the ability *to feel*."

✳✳✳

"Griffin, I've figured out the power source that we need for the machine."

Griffin pauses his work on his tablet to turn around and face Evander. "Oh really? I hope it's nothing too difficult to obtain…"

Evander sighs. "it's uranium."

"What?"

"Yeah, it's a chemical compound found on Earth that, unbeknownst to humanoids, actually has the power to bend time and alternate universes. It's commonly used thematically in their recreational entertainment films, but it actually does what they portray it as. On an unrelated note, they also use it in nuclear warfare, but that's a story for another day."

Griffin rests his head on his desk for a moment. He's been up working for hours, with very little to no rest. "Okay, so how do we get it?"

Evander sighs. "I'm still working that part out. The difficult thing about it, is that it exists only in small quantities on Earth - and it's so rare that most of the existing quantities are kept under lock and key."

"Okay, so what does that mean for us, exactly?" Griffin begins nervously tapping his fingers on his desk, clearly wanting Evander to get to the point and to stop dancing around it.

"We're going to have to travel to Earth…"

"Yeah, and then what?"

"We'll have to go to a lab and steal it."

CHAPTER 5

Luna leaves the Grand Hall the way she always does after a visit with Onyx - happy to have had some tie with him, but quite dejected and frustrated that he's still stuck there against his will. The whole thing had gotten so messy - and fixing it was even more unwieldy.

"Hello, Luna. How are you holding up?"

Luna turns mid-stride to see Vidia, another sorter, catch up with her. "Oh, you know, business as usual. I was just visiting Onyx and…"

"Oh my pod I can only imagine how difficult that must have been for you! I mean, it has been a difficult time for you, overall."

"It really has been, yes. But now I was just about to get back to work so…"

"I mean you two are so perfect for each other. At least, I think so. I don't feel emotions the way you two do, of course. You're a special pair indeed." Vidia glosses over Luna's attempt to make a hasty getaway with a sassy smirk and a friendly wink. It's not that Luna dislikes Vidia - rather, she just gets tired of being reminded about Onyx every second of every waking moment. She is tortured enough from her own psyche and its accompanying emotions, that any external reminders from others, while well-meaning, can feel excessive and potentially make things worse.

"Yes, he really is wonderful. Now, I'm just going to head back to work so I'll see you later?" Luna forces the words out in a hurry to keep Vidia from interrupting her again.

"Oh, for sure! Perhaps we can meet after your shift?"

Luna tries her best to hide the pained expression threatening to spread across her face. After finishing her shift, she was planning to just curl up and cry for a while in her pod - that is, until Vidia mentioned other plans.

"Today isn't the best day for that. I really just need some time to process everything. I hope you'll understand."

"Oh you don't understand it yet? Let me explain! So Onyx is stuck on the throne because-"

"Vidia!" Luna puts a hand up to stop her from rehashing what she's been trying to forget. "I'm clear on what happened. I just mean I'm emotionally spent and need some time to work through that."

Vidia's lips make a rounded "o" shape, and then she politely nods and walks past her to wherever she was going. Luna exhales a breath she didn't even realize she was holding. The thing about having emotions in a place where the vast majority of beings do not, is that explaining yourself and your unique needs to them is difficult and sometimes impossible - because they simply do not have the capacity to relate. But Luna comforts herself with the knowledge that this is only temporary - an impermanent state of affairs that will dissipate once Onyx is freed. That's what she hopes, anyway.

✳✳✳

"What do you mean we have to steal it?" Griffin's eyes go wide at Evander's brash suggestion.

"I mean, we're going to go to Earth, enter a lab containing uranium, and bring back enough of it to power the time machine."

"You sound insane."

Evander opens his mouth, and then closes it to avoid snapping back at the words of his younger protegé. "Well, do you have any better ideas? We have someone stuck on a chair whose morale is rapidly weakening. We gotta get him off that chair. Luna is a mess too, you know. I don't understand these emotions, but anyone can see she's in pain."

Griffin dejectedly nods, likely a bit embarrassed at his own outburst. "I know, it's just… we don't usually resort to thievery. It's not ideal."

"That is true - especially when it's the inter-dimensional kind which is especially frowned-upon. But we are fresh out of options at the moment. I'd suggest you ready yourself to go to Earth. I've reserved the transport room for us shortly."

Griffin exhales sharply and shrugs. "Okay, I guess that's that then. You're coming with me though, right?"

Evander nods. "Of course. I wouldn't send you there alone - at least not yet."

That last part of the sentence leaves Griffin with many unanswered questions, but he comforts himself with

26

the overarching thought that Evander is only looking out for his best interest - even if it doesn't make sense upon first glance.

"Evander, where exactly, will you be taking us on Earth? Is there a specific lab you had in mind?"

Evander smiles at Griffin's simplistic question. "Absolutely, yes. I have done some research and found a lab with the lowest security measures."

"Oh good - so we don't have to worry about sneaking in and taking it?"

Evander rolls his eyes. "There is still going to be security measures in place, just *less* than other labs, in comparison. I'm bringing a small canister that will be safe to store it in. And as long as I place the canister in the pocket of my jumpsuit, it will come with us in between dimensions."

"Well, this is quite a bit over my head, but I trust you, Evander. I'll meet you at the transport room shortly."

CHAPTER 6

Luna finishes her shift in the Sorting Room for the day, and makes her way back to her pod after clocking out. The hazy, purple environment of the Upperworld seems to swirl around her as she walks, the tepid temperature strangely comforting and soothing to her frazzled nerves. She's starving for affection, and no one here can provide that for her as they simply just don't understand how she feels, because they're numb. Hopelessly numb, all of them.

Except for Onyx, that is. Just her luck that the only one who can understand her in this realm is imprisoned by his prestige. And they both need each other - desperately. Being alone is breaking them, both physically and emotionally.

Evander and Griffin are going to fix this. I trust them completely. They'll do whatever it takes to get him away from that wretched chair.

Luna hugs one of her throw pillows to her chest as she sinks into her plush bed. She already took a small nap earlier, but another certainly couldn't hurt. She watches the Upperworld beings go by through the window of her pod as even sleep abandons her.

Is it better to be completely numb, like the others? Or should I be glad I can feel? Right now it seems like a disadvantage to need things the way I do. I bet Onyx can relate to that. I hate that he is stuck there. It's just completely and totally unfair. Onyx has done so much for

28

everyone, and yet this was still asked of him. I don't regret that he saved everyone, I just wish it didn't have to be him that did the saving.

The troublesome thoughts continue to swirl around her head, and without the energy to fight them, Luna leaves them be. It's unnecessarily difficult and complicated to fight a war within yourself. And it's extra difficult when you're the only one fighting it.

✳✳✳

Griffin blinks rapidly as his own body reassembles itself, piece by piece, in the middle of a grassy field hidden by the underbrush. He sits up, and takes in the unique surroundings of what he is realizing is Earth.

"Evander? Are you here?" He looks around for his companion, and finds him sitting just a few feet away from him on the grass.

"I'm right here, don't worry." Evander also seems to be reacting to the differing atmospheric pressure, as he too is struggling to get up from his seated posture.

"Why is it harder to move?" Griffin groans as he slowly finds his way onto his feet, but grabs hold of a nearby tree trunk for support.

"There is a lot more gravitational pull in this dimension - more than what we are used to, especially on this planet. At least, that's what my research suggested. I'm not an expert on Earth life the way Onyx is - I didn't have to study it as in-depth as he did."

Griffin nods, and starts to steady himself on his feet without support. "Okay, so where is this lab we're getting the uranium from?"

Evander steps closer to him and lowers his voice. "Should be near here, I'm tracking the location on my embedded device. Speaking of which, our bodies will expel our devices if we remain here for more than twenty-four Earth hours, so we've got to get in, and get right out."

"Expel it? Why?"

"It's a safety feature - in rare cases, when an Upperworld being ends up staying on Earth permanently, getting rid of the technology is important as to not raise suspicions. That is, unless you'd prefer to become a glorified lab rat."

"What?"

Evander sighs. "Don't worry about it. Let's just go - we have plenty of time but we must stay on schedule."

The two walk in silence for a few moments until Griffin speaks up. "So, where are we, anyway?"

Evander pauses to take in the unique scenery of the blue atmosphere and the green foliage. "We're in New Mexico, a portion of the United States of America."

Griffin nods, even though that answer doesn't totally give him much insight into anything useful. "Okay. So, what's the plan?"

Evander nods his head in the direction of the large building they are approaching. "I have arranged for us to be let through the main entrance by my Upperworld contact. His name is Ronald Emerson, and he'll get us through the first layer of security. After that, we are unfortunately, on our own.

Griffin gulps slowly, readying himself for the task at hand. "Okay, so I guess I'll just follow your lead then."

"Sounds good."

The two make their way toward the entrance of the building, under a pristinely-power washed outdoor sign emblazoned with the words "McGill Labs". The green and beige elements of the logo seem to imply that the inner workings of that organization is relatively natural and good for the planet, which seems quite ironic, as it's likely not.

"Ready for this? You're going to have to move fast, and move accurately. Follow my directions exactly, and do not hesitate. Do not look back. Understand me?" Evander looks at Griffin with a steely sort of focus and desperation.

"I understand. Let's do this."

CHAPTER 7

Luna awakens from her slumber with the door to her pod beeping. Clearly, someone wants to come in. She gets up, and shuffles directly to the door.

"Vidia, I thought I told you I wasn't up for anything today - Oh, Brielle, I'm sorry. I thought you were..."

"Vidia? No, sorry." Brielle fiddles nervously with a few strands of her shiny, metallic hair and seems to be actually regretful of her unannounced presence.

"No, don't worry about it, I just meant that..." Luna stops herself from trying to explain away the human tendencies that she had picked up during her time on Earth. It has become abundantly clear that not only to Upperworld beings lack the capacity to understand or relate, but trying to explain it only makes things even more awkward. "Just come on in."

Brielle nods apologetically and follows Luna back into her pod. Her pillows and bedsheets are strewn everywhere, as it's clear that Luna has been feeling ill at ease.

"Are you doing okay? I came by to check on you. I just figured... you could use a friend." Brielle smiles sweetly and gestures to a small canister that she brought with her. "I just brewed some of my special passionfruit tea, maybe it'll relax you a bit?"

Luna smiles, and even though she knows it won't really make much of a difference, accepts the canister gratefully and takes a sip. "Well, this is really good anyway, Brielle. Thank you very much."

"My pleasure, Luna. Me and a lot of the others… we're all worried about you. I wish we could help somehow."

"You *are* helping. Even if it doesn't seem like it, I really do appreciate you." Luna pats her on the shoulder and then settles on one of the chairs at her small pod dining table. Brielle follows and sits across from her.

"He'll make it out of this, you know. I just know it."

Luna sighs. "I sure hope so. I'm trying not to get my hopes up, but hope is so very tempting, especially when I have very little else to go on."

A potentially awkward silence threatens to make the visit awkward, but Brielle manages to think of something to say. "So, you and Onyx are… something, right? I know you have some sort of connection that I can't quite understand, but I knew something was up with you two."

Luna sighs and looks out the pod window. "Yes, it's a very long and twisted story - a story that goes back a lot further than I have any capability of remembering…"

Brielle's bright eyes widen in anticipation and intrigue. "Well, I have time, and I do love a good story…"

Luna takes a deep breath, and then recounts everything that Onyx had explained to her. She tries (and fails) to hide the way her cheeks warm and her pulse quickens at the remembrance of that morning in their Earthly home when all was explained to her.

✳✳✳

"Ronald will be right through this door. Follow my lead, and don't arouse suspicions to anyone around us." Griffin nods, and follows Evander through the door.

"Hello, we're here to look into the *electrical wiring issue*." Recognition floods Ronald's face, as he pushes his black-rimmed glasses further onto his nose and leads the two men over to a controlled-access door.

"Glad you could make it as soon as you did. We've been having a lot of trouble with *our automatic docking system* lately. Glad it's going to be all fixed now."

Evander nods, satisfied that the code words were received smoothly. Then he walks past Ronald through the door he opened, with Griffin in tow. The two walk calmly down a labyrinth of hallways and various other doors, until they reach a room deep in the sterile atmosphere of the lab that appears to be under heavy surveillance and limited clearance.

"Griffin, I need you to disable the security cameras. I'm going to hack into this digital keypad system so we can get into the door. Per my limited research, there may be some laser detection as well, so disable those also unless you want to have to jump through literal hoops to get what we need."

Griffin nods and walks a few paces down the hall to the first visible surveillance camera. With a few flicks of his wrist and some amateur fiddling, he manages to disable the camera, and then remotely disable the others monitoring the room with the uranium in it. As soon as he finishes with the last camera, he turns to walk back toward Evander, but sirens begin to blare, and he freezes.

"We've been detected! Hurry, get in NOW!"

Griffin follows suit without protest, but he starts to shake a little under the extreme panic he feels himself descending into. "What do we do know?"

"We have no choice but to grab it and go. Find it, quickly!!!" The two hear invisible footsteps rapidly following them from the other end of the hallway, and dive right into the task at hand. Across the room, both their eyes land on a plethora of yellow caution signs surrounding a separated area of the back of the room. The signs read "Caution: radioactive uranium ore" and seems to be suggesting the reader to put on a nearby safety suit before entering the vicinity of the uranium. Evander notices Griffin's hesitation but quickly negates the cautionary tale.

"We don't have time, just let me get in there!" Evander removes the sample collector out of his own suit and opens the tank holding the uranium when they are stopped by some loud voices behind them.

"STOP RIGHT THERE AND KEEP YOUR HANDS WHERE I CAN SEE THEM!"

CHAPTER 8

"Wow, that's really... interesting." Brielle seems thoroughly captivated by Luna's storytelling, but is of course, rendered unable to react emotionally. Luna, on the other hand, is left teary-eyed after recollecting in detail all that has occurred between her and Onyx. Of course, she left out plenty of the more intimate details of their relationship, but even the basic overview left her wildly emotional and wistful.

"That's one way to put it, for sure." Luna sighs for likely the hundredth time that day. "So that's the story, and now you know."

Brielle nods. "Well, I hope I didn't seem nosy. But it helps to understand a bit more about what happened. Have you gotten to talk to Onyx at all lately?"

Luna smiles as sadly as possible while still smiling. "Only just about every chance I get. That is, when I'm not working my shift or crying myself to sleep in here."

Brielle tilts her head in confusion. "'Crying'? what is 'crying'?"

"It's..." Luna begins to try to explain it but then catches herself before wasting her breath. "... not anything you need to worry about it. Just an outpouring of emotion that humanoids experience sometimes."

She nods but still seems curious. "Part of me wishes that I could relate to what you're describing more deeply, but at the same time, feelings seem like a lot more trouble than they're worth."

"Well said, my friend. Well said. And you are absolutely right."

✳✳✳

Evander and Griffin exchange troubled glances, but they quickly realize that one of them has to act fast before they are overtaken by the security guards.

"Stay very still, and very calm, and no one gets hurt." The words fall slowly out of the guard's mouth, oozing through the dry air of the lab and clawing its way into their ears. The potential of what "getting hurt" means in this context could spell disaster for this brave duo.

Evander manages to signal Griffin just slightly, with their previously agreed-upon signal: a double wink. That means that Griffin will create a diversion while Evander would be expected to collect the sample.

After a strategic and silent count to five, Griffin smoothly sweeps the legs out from under the nearest security guard.

"Restrain him immediately!" The attention of the other guards quickly moves to both Griffin and the guard he has upended while Evander runs straight into the toxic surroundings of the uranium. He quickly reaches in with the protective gloves he hid in his jumpsuit pocket, and then places a large enough chunk of it into his sample collector.

"HEY, WHAT ARE YOU DOING?"

The guards swiftly walk toward Griffin from across the room, but Evander manages to free himself long enough to grab Griffin's arm and head back to the hallway. The guards try to catch up to them, but they can't due to the bunch of chairs Griffin threw in their way from an adjacent alcove housing a rolling cart full of folding chairs. Having dumped them all on the floor, they made a reasonably good deterrent, giving both Evander and Griffin just long enough to get back through the main door and into the main lobby of the lab.

"Thanks again, Ronald, for your help. We've gotta transport back up now."

He nods silently before pointing a small hand-held device at them and pressing a small button on the side just as the door bursts open. But the guards are too late - Evander and Griffin are already gone, back up to the Upperworld where they belong.

CHAPTER 9

Both Evander and Griffin's cells reassemble in the Upperworld, just after narrowly escaping arrest in McGill labs. Both of their chests are heaving on the transport tables they reanimated on, as the subtle buzzing and winding of the transport room machines powers down.

"You got it?" Griffin looks over to Evander hopefully.

"Oh, I got it all right." Evander removes the sample collector from out of his zippered pocket. The uranium has an eerie greenish glow in its container, which lights up the dim lighting around it and bounces off of their excited faces.

"It certainly looks... powerful", Griffin observes. Evander nods, as he places the sample back in his pocket.

"And one sample that size is enough?"

"Should be - according to my calculations, anyway. This stuff is so full of raw inter-dimensional energy that just a measly crumb of it is probably enough. We should have more than enough."

The two have trouble hiding the smiles on their faces as they recover and regroup from their brief trip to Earth.

"I don't know why people live on Earth. The air scrapes your throat as it goes down, and it's a lot harder to move." Griffin rubs the back of his neck while remembering his first-time experience in a heavier gravitational pull.

"Well, it's not like humanoids really have a choice… it's just kind of where they end up."

"I suppose, but I am extremely grateful I'm not one of them. And then there's all the hustle and bustle and responsibilities… I wouldn't want any of that."

"We do have responsibilities here too, of course." Evander smirks as he eases himself off the table.

Griffin nods, but seems to relate to that fact differently than Evander does. He shrugs, and opens his mouth much wider than necessary to speak, as if he was caught mid-thought. "True, but it doesn't feel the same. Not that I got a full sense of things on Earth during our very brief escapade, but from what I heard and what little I did see, humanoids seem utterly obsessed with the daily hustle. No wonder they age so fast and die so young."

Evander sighs. "Immortals are very much like that - they have a very real trouble staying focused in the here-and-now, rather, they like to plan ahead all the time. Like I always like to say - there's no time like the present. Literally. Because the past is long gone and the future never really exists, if you think about it."

Griffin nods slowly, in awe of the wisdom of his more experienced counterpart. "I never really thought of it that way - that is, quite insightful indeed."

Evander nods and then clears his throat. "So, are you ready to build this thing? How are your blueprints coming?"

"Well, I'm still working out the kinks and collecting materials. I've made a preliminary list. Perhaps I should send it over to you?"

"Certainly. That way I can start to collect things as well - thank you for your attention to detail and diligence, Griffin. It wouldn't be possible without you - and I am sure that both Luna and Onyx will be forever in your debt if we can pull this off."

"What happens if we can't?"

Both men pause momentarily, clearly at a loss for words, until Evander breaks the silence. "Well, truth be told, I really don't know what would happen. This is uncharted territory, so I don't have any records to refer to. But perhaps it might be worth me looking into a sort of 'plan B' should this not go as planned."

"It might be worth doing some digging, maybe to see if there's anything we're overlooking in this process. It would be a disaster if something bad started happening right under our noses."

Evander nods. "Okay, I'll take that upon myself to look into - you should just keep on working with the blueprints and supply lists so we can build it sooner versus later."

Griffin nods. "And the uranium - you'll keep it safe?"

Evander nods. "Absolutely."

✳✳✳

After yet another long shift spent in the Sorting Room, Luna makes her customary visit to see Onyx. She's gotten it down to a pretty regimented routine at this point - the organized scheduling gives her something to hold onto. The one who always kept her safe and secure up until this point is unable to do so, which means that Luna has slowly but steadily learned how to care for and soothe herself. That is, with a little help from some of her friends whenever they come around.

"Hello, my love." His weary voice echoes with a newfound strength across the sublime acoustics of the Grand Hall. Luna approaches him the same way she always does - with a smile plastered across her face and her long, dark hair pulled back into a ponytail as she's been working hard as of late.

"Hello, Onyx." She makes herself comfortable on the much smaller chair that has been placed for her at the foot of Onyx's throne. Her chair also ensures that she doesn't accidentally forget the danger Onyx possesses and she get too close to him.

"I hear that Griffin and Evander are hard at work trying to help me get off this thing."

Luna nods. "Indeed! They actually went to Earth to get some sort of materials for the machine. They're doing everything they possibly can for you... for us." She forces herself to smile in the midst of the agony she feels, but something about it feels fake. Luna then tilts her head up to meet Onyx's gaze, and she notices that his eyes and hair are now glowing, and very brightly.

"You're… really glowing now, Onyx. Are you sure that's okay and not dangerous for you?"

Onyx shrugs, the subtle flames of his bleach-blonde hair waving in response. "I mean, I just assumed everything was under control. I'd like to believe that, since I don't really have a choice, regardless."

"That may be so, but I might ask around just to make sure. I don't know what I'd do if -"
Luna stops herself from completing that thought, as she knows that nothing good would happen from worrying him too much.

"Okay, well that's up to you. Please don't concern yourself with me. I'm holding up all right, really. In fact, I've almost… come to like it."

Luna rolls her eyes. She can detect what humanoids call "BS" from a mile away. "Onyx, I don't want you to pretend for me. I know that you're suffering and in dire need of relief."

His shoulders slump at the realization of her words, and the smile he plastered on is rapidly washed away by his tears. Even his flaming hair seems to dim a little.

"You're absolutely right, Luna. Okay, I'll be honest with you." He sighs and hesitates before continuing. "Not only is this mentally daunting and difficult to be without you, but it's hurting my body as well. It hurts to sit here as long as I have, and I can't even physically move to shift my weight. My eyesight isn't as good as it used to be, probably something about the light behind them making it harder for my corneas to absorb and detect light. And my scalp is literally *on fire* but I can't do anything about it. I can't touch it - heck, I can't even scream. Something about this chair has made my pulse rate lower considerably so I feel very, very weak. That's the ugly truth, Luna. Is that what you wanted?"

Luna's face turns bright red and she starts shaking uncontrollably. She sobs loudly into her palms, and Onyx immediately regrets being so harsh with her.

"Luna, I'm... so sorry. I just... had to tell someone. I shouldn't have snapped at you like that. I'm sorry..."

She turns to leave, running out of the Grand Hall in a pile of tears and panic. "No, Luna, please don't leave. Luna. LUNA!"

But his cries fall on deaf ears.

CHAPTER 10

Griffin heads back to his office to mark uranium off of the supply list. Over the past few shift changes, he has been able to collect just about everything else on the list, like the external materials and some more rudimentary things like nuts, bolts, and screws.

He looks outside the window of his office at the Upperworld outside it, with its sprawling idyllic landscape with the typical lavender fog hovering above it all. He sighs, thinking about how tough and dangerous this endeavor truly is. His hands are quite gifted, as they have such a clear connection to his brain. He's easily one of the best techs and mechanics that the Upperworld currently has in its arsenal - and yet he still doubts himself almost every moment of every day.

Griffin gets up from his desk and moves to pick through the large box of supplies he has collected. After selecting a few pieces of what he has deemed usable scrap metal, he picks up his welding mask and gets to work. The fiery brightness of his torch creates a stark contrast to the otherwise sterile and calm aesthetic of the record-keeping office, with its quiet pulsing lights and state-of-the-art technology. As the first piece of metal welds together with the piece he held up to it at just the right angle, a small smile of hope slides across his mouth, as he realizes that maybe there's a chance that their borderline crazy, time-warping plan may just work after all.

He works diligently for a long time after that, building at least the outer frame of the time machine to his liking - that's the easy part. The inner workings of the machine, including the mechanization of the uranium, would have to be left for his wiser mentor, Evander. As skilled as Griffin is, he doesn't waste time or energy denying the indubitable truth that Evander is the one to handle the more intricately sensitive elements of the machine. Also, Griffin knows that although they have collected a good amount of uranium, it is not unlimited, and wasting it during frivolous experimentation is not an option.

After what feels like forever, Griffin steps back, and wipes the sweat off of his face that had mingled with the grime leftover from his welding mask. He takes off his very sweaty shirt, as the rubbery Upperworld garments are many things, but breathable is not one of them. Griffin finds a nearby towel that he must have left on his chair earlier, and towel dries himself until he can get home to his pod for a proper shower later.

Once he refocuses on his task at hand, he smiles to himself, taking in his stellar accomplishment - the outer frame of the time machine, and all its visible outer components, are complete. Even the wearable bracelet for the brave time traveler has been completed - so that they can zap themselves back to the Upperworld whenever they are finished. It's far from finished, of course, but getting closer. He sighs to himself in relief.

Well, I've done my part. It's time for Evander to take over now. I sure hope he knows how to use that uranium, because I sure don't.

✳✳✳

Evander brings the uranium back to his pod so he can lock it in the little safe he installed under the table of his kitchenette. He fishes the key out of the small flower pot where he always hides it, and inserts the key into the lock, turning until it opens. The little door gives way to his gentle tugging, until he is met with the mostly empty inside of the blue velvet furnished safe. He sees the top-secret envelopes holding his various other personal effects, such as his personal formulas and unprotected blueprints. Evander reaches into the zippered pocket of his jumpsuit and retrieves the collection container holding the vaguely green-glow of the uranium sample. Holding the tube momentarily in his hand, he can feel the energy flowing through the piece of the radioactive rock that he broke off of the larger batch in the Earth lab. Smiling to himself, he places it gingerly next to the neatly-piled blueprints and personal effects, noticing that the sample appears even brighter in the darker confines of the safe. The green glow of the uranium mixes with the blue sheen of the velvet, creating a rather swampy aqua sort of color. He closes the door of the safe and swiftly locks it tightly again, feeling fairly confident that the all-important sample will be left untouched.

After replacing the tablecloth on the table, Evander makes his way over to his couch. he grabs his tablet off of his side table to catch up on the latest in Upperworld news, as well as some Earth current events. It's always good to be informed about the state of affairs in the world of the lives they touch, he always thinks to himself.

Shortly after finishing his typical rounds on the technological news scape, Evander remembers his conversation with Griffin about doing some research about the whole situation Onyx is in and what would happen if they are unsuccessful in their time machine endeavor. He shivers, as he knows that they must find out one way or another, but this sort of information is usually hard to find and even harder to swallow. He takes a sip of water from his nearby glass and shakes off any apprehension he feels about it in the name of necessity and scientific exploration.

He begins by using his tablet to log into the archives of the Upperworld, with his unique PIN number and passcode. Then he begins searching for the more esoteric information surrounding the throne and how the energy current flows through it. More specifically, Evander hopes to find information about how the one seated on the throne is affected by the current over time and if there are any side effects or issues that they may have overlooked in their feverish search for a replacement.

After flipping through some articles and records, he sees what appears to be one of the first photographs of Zephyr taken when he was on the throne. Evander shrugs and keeps flipping through the other records, until it hits him - Zephyr looks a lot more human-like than he did in the centuries when Evander was around to see him. His skin had a lot more color in it, his hair sat more naturally on his head, and his eyes didn't glow at all - and neither did his hair.

Evander's eyes widen, and he drops his glass of water on the floor as the realization hits him. He doesn't bother to clean up the shards of glass - instead, he runs out of his pod, carrying his tablet in his hands. He has to speak to Luna, and *fast*.

CHAPTER 11

"Luna? Luna! I have to speak with you immediately. Where are you?" Evander hits the door notification button on the outside wall of her pod repeatedly, but she doesn't seem to be home.

This is bad, this is really, really bad. How am I going to explain this to her? I don't want to worry her, but she has a right to know. Where could she possibly be?

Evander decides to walk around a bit and look for her or someone who would know where she is. The tepid air of the Upperworld makes him sweat in his feverish state as he paces around the radius of her pod. *Luna, where are you?*

He is about to give up his manual search and just call her on her embedded device, until he remembers that she lost hers on Earth a while ago and it hasn't yet been replaced, at least to his knowledge, anyway. Evander is about to launch into full-out panic mode, that is, until he sees a flash of bright fuchsia hair pass by near him.

"Vidia? Vidia!" She turns immediately upon hearing her name, her typical smile turning into a concerned frown.

"Evander, is everything all right? What is going on?"

He struggles to catch his breath after having rushed around in pursuit of Luna. "I'm looking for Luna, but I haven't seen her anywhere. Do you know where I can find her? It is of utmost importance."

"I haven't seen her too recently, but I know that a while ago, she ran right out of the Grand Hall crying. I have no idea about what, and I was a bit concerned too but she ran right past me. I never even got the chance to check on her."

Evander nods disappointedly. "Okay, well if you happen to see her, do tell her to come find me."

"Why didn't you just call her on her device?"

"I don't think she ever had it replaced after it was expelled on Earth."

Vidia nods and sighs. "Well, I'll let someone know about that and have it looked into. It should have been replaced ages ago." She makes a quick note on the tablet she carries around with her just about everywhere. "I'll have to let the medical department know and maybe have the procedure scheduled for her."

"That's not really priority right now, Vidia, trust me when I say there are *much* more pressing matters at hand."

Vidia places a manicured hand on her hip. "Do you seriously mean to tell me that an untracked, unreachable sorter is not priority? She needs to be able to be reached at all times, to prevent issues like this," she motions toward Evander, "from occurring."

Evander manages to steady his breathing long enough to find Luna. "I don't have the time or the patience to question you right now, Vidia, so I'm just going to continue on my way. Please do tell her to find me as soon as she can. Thanks!"

Vidia mumbles something under her breath but Evander is too far away to hear it. He continues looking for Luna, until he sees her sitting at the base of the fountain in the middle of the socialization area of the Upperworld. No one seems to notice her there, as most sorters and record keepers are completely unaware of emotions and their effects on humanoids. Evander had to educate himself on it to even somewhat understand - and he knows that he never fully will. She has her knees drawn up to her chest, and appears to be watching the other beings go about their business while she cries. Evander sighs, knowing that the news he has is not going to make her feel any better, but decides that it is likely best she knows sooner versus later.

"Hello there, Luna." She pauses sobbing just long enough to meet Evander's kind gaze from under her disheveled, dark black hair.

"Hi Evander."

He swallows a bit before continuing, as he knows that the truth is going to hit her hard - and it looks like something else already did.

"So, are you all right, Luna? What is the matter?"

She sniffles and then looks down at her feet. "It's Onyx. I just visited him and he... he yelled at me. He's never been upset with me before. It really hurt." Evander sighs, and then squats down to pat her on the back awkwardly. He quickly decides that whatever she is feeling might as well be handled before he drops this hard truth onto her.

"Oh really? What were you talking about that upset him?" Luna starts sobbing again, and starts to lean more heavily on Evander's shoulder.

"I wanted to make sure he was doing okay with everything, despite the unfortunate circumstances. And it turns out... he was lying to me the whole time. He's not doing okay at all!"

Evander freezes. "What exactly do you mean?"

Luna tries to catch her breath between cries, and Evander gently brushes a few unruly strands of her hair out of her face. He's gotten a bit better at comforting her, but Onyx is really the only one who can completely make her feel better - because he understands what emotions can do to a person better than anyone else.

"That chair is hurting him. He said his hair is burning him, he cannot see well, and his body hurts from sitting for as long as he has. And there's nothing I can do to help him at all!" Luna continues crying almost uncontrollably, and Evander is scared nearly motionless. It appears that Luna is noticing exactly what he was afraid of - that the chair is *changing* Onyx, and not for the better.

"Luna, I don't want to scare you any further, but I found some things that could explain why that is happening."

She stops sobbing only long enough to lock eyes with Evander, and then to chance a glance at the tablet he holds in his hand.

"I found some things about Zephyr that seem to be the reason for this. Take a look at this very old picture of Zephyr."

Her eyes widen as she notices Zephyr looking a lot different than she would expect. "That was really him?" Evander nods.

"Yes, that was Zephyr during his earlier days on the throne. Before... the current truly took hold of him."

"And after?"

Evander flips forward to a different image, one that was taken of Zephyr much later. "Indeed - this is how I was used to seeing him, and I honestly thought he always looked like this. Unfortunately, I was very, very wrong."

Luna pauses, still wiping tears from her face on the back of her sleeve. "So this means..." She has trouble getting the words out of her mouth, so Evander takes the liberty of saying them for her.

"Onyx will start to degrade as well, just like this. In fact, it seems he already started."

CHAPTER 12

Griffin sits back admiring his work with the machine, just as the door beeps to signal a visitor is waiting. He gets up to let them in, and opens the door to be met with Evander's worried face.

"Hello Evander. I made some great progress with the machine - the entire outer casing has been finished, now we just have to get the inside to work. Oh, is something wrong?" He reacts immediately to Evander's obvious discomfort.

"Well, you see, there *is* indeed something that we seem to have overlooked. And it is something quite important."

Griffin raises a concerned eyebrow. "Oh? How so?"

"Well, it turns out that Onyx is degenerating from the presence of the current coursing through him. We have proof that the same thing happened to Zephyr over eons."

Griffin scratches his head. "Well that's just it - you said it happened to Zephyr over eons. The way you're talking, it sounds as if it's happening a lot faster with Onyx."

Evander nods. "Exactly. And I wish I had a definite answer as to why, but I honestly have no idea. I guess it is possible that since Onyx is part humanoid, perhaps the current will affect him at a different rate. There really is no way to know for sure though."

The two stand in silence for a moment, pondering the conundrum they seemingly have gotten themselves into. Neither one of them wants any permanent damage to happen to Onyx. But right now, they are nearly fresh out of ideas.

"Well, it seems that the only option we really have, is to just go about our business as planned and hope it works."

Griffin moves toward the time machine that he's been working on. Evander follows, interested in seeing his progress with it so far.

"This is very impressive! The form feels very strong, and I am pleased with the way it's been welded together. I appreciate your efforts, Griffin. Excellent work."

"Thank you. Now, this is where my expertise ends. I have no idea how to implement the use of uranium."

Evander pauses, and pats him on the shoulder. "I understand that maybe you are unfamiliar with the process, but I myself only know a little bit about it. So, I will be needing your assistance throughout the binding process."

"Really? You want *my* help?"

"Of course! Why wouldn't I?"

"Well, I often just don't feel… intelligent enough. I've worked hard to learn all that I can, both through research, and from you. But I still doubt myself, quite often."

Evander pats him reassuringly on the back. "But your intelligence comes from the fact that you are willing to learn. Ability to adapt to any given circumstance is the true measure of knowledge - and you have already shown yourself to be quite flexible in various different situations. Trust your inner voice, and your natural instinctual propensities. You have what it takes, Griffin. And you are quite gifted, truly."

He smiles at his younger protégé. "I'll get the uranium sample from my pod, and then... let's finish this time machine."

✳✳✳

Luna continues to cry until all her tears run out, and then she begins the walk back to her pod to take a nap. She walks through the hazy purple fog, feeling numb, as the dull sting in the pit of her stomach begins to subside only because it is constant and her body begins to block it out. She makes it almost there until Vidia catches up with her.

"Luna! There you are!"

Luna stops in her tracks, her tear-stained face turning around to meet Vidia's nonchalant gaze.

"Hi Vidia. Look, I really need to get back to my pod to get some sleep..."

"But Luna, you have to understand, this is important." She places her hand on her hip. "I had heard from Evander that it seems you're still missing your device?"

Luna nods. "Yes, but I don't miss it. Everyone knows where to find me, either in my pod or in the Sorting Room."

"Unfortunately, that is no longer enough. Evander was looking for you, and couldn't find you."

"But he did find me, I was near the water fountain."

"That's not good enough, Luna. I have made arrangements for you at the medical office to get another device implanted in your wrist."

"Thank you, but I really don't need it."

"Luna, you know that it is Upperworld policy for everyone to be tracked at all times. It is how we run things so smoothly here."

"Oh, I didn't realize. I thought I would be an exception, given the circumstances."

Vidia shakes her head. "No, unfortunately not. Please do come with me."

Luna reluctantly follows her. "Will it… hurt?"

Vidia shakes her head. No, not at all. The area will be put under localized anesthetic. You won't feel a thing. It's a less common procedure, as there aren't too many sorters who have lost their implant on Earth, but it does happen occasionally. We usually try to replace it as soon as they return, although I think we really dropped the ball on this one. For that, I apologize."

Luna nods politely, not truly sure how to respond to that. She follows Vidia toward the medical office calmly, even though the idea of the surgery terrifies her.

"Right this way, Luna." Vidia points to a medical aid who stands at the front desk with a tablet.

"Hello Sage, I have Luna here for her implant replacement."

The medical office aid taps on her tablet and then nods. "Yes, perfect. She can take a seat, I'll have a doctor see her momentarily."

Vidia nods her thanks. "Alright Luna, I have things to do, so you'll have take it from here. You'll be fine, Doctor Amaranthus is one of the best we have. Don't worry!" Vidia smiles at her, and then breezes out through the front door.

Luna sighs, clearly not wanting to be here doing this, but she doesn't see any real way around it.

"Hello, Luna? I'm Doctor Amaranthus. I've heard so much about you. Come along, let's get you prepped."

She looks up to see a kindly looking older being, with medium brown hair and bright eyes.

"Hello." She shifts uncomfortable in her seat surrounded by the very basic and sterile furnishings of the medical office.

"There's no need to worry, come with me."

She reluctantly gets up to follow the doctor, who leads her into an operating room.

"Please lay down and I will apply the anesthetic."

Luna does as she is told, while trying to content herself by looking up at the very bland ceiling.

"I'm going to inject your wrist with the anesthetic so you won't feel a thing, and then I'll make a slight incision to deposit your implant. There have been upgrades, since you've been gone. The new ones have wireless internet now, isn't that nice?" The doctor's attempt to lighten the mood go unnoticed, as Luna only has enough energy to look at him with a very dead stare. "I don't blame you one bit, actually. This whole thing is kind of unnecessary. But, rules are rules, of course. And I hate to scar your lovely, healthy skin, but I suppose is must be done."

The doctor pauses before picking up his scalpel. "I'd suggest you look away now. I promise you won't feel any pain."

Luna turns her head slightly away, but still braces herself for the pain of the cut, even though it never comes. A bit of pressure on her wrist is all it is, and then it's over as quickly as it began.

CHAPTER 13

"You're sure you know what you're doing with that?" Griffin looks quizzically at Evander as he holds the uranium sample in his bare hands.

"No, not entirely. But I know enough." He brings it toward the time machine, and looks for the appropriate place to deposit it.

"Griffin, can you hand me that wrench over there, by any chance?"

Griffin moves to get the wrench, but somehow, it rises into the air on its own. He rubs his eyes, thinking perhaps he just needs some sleep. "Evander, I think I need a nap. I think I'm overtired, because I just saw that wrench levitate."

Evander turns his head in that direction, and watches in shock as the wrench floats directly over to him and lands in his hand. "What in the Underworld just happened?"

Griffin freezes in pure terror. "I... have no idea. Did you just... did you make it float like that?"

Evander pauses, and puts the uranium down, back into its protective case. "I don't know... I didn't mean to, anyway. Did you?"

"What? How would I have done that?"

"Well, how did *I* do it then?"

Both men are quite spooked at this anomaly that occurred, but that is nothing compared to what is about to happen. They catch their breath and steady themselves, long enough to have a drink of water.

"Thanks, Griffin."

"For what?"

"The water. You got me a glass of water."

"What? No I didn't. I've been right here the whole time."

"Well, if you didn't, then who did?"

The two of them gingerly turn around to see the pitcher of water moving, seemingly of its own accord, through the air and back to the counter where it belongs.

"I, think we're losing our minds, Evander." Griffin sits down on the nearby chair, resting his head in his hands. "I can't process this. There's no sense to be made."

Evander opens his mouth to speak, but then it comes to him. "Don't admit yourself to the psych office just yet. I think I know what happened."

"Really? How in the universe are you going to explain this?"

Evander wastes no time, and picks up the container of uranium on the countertop. "Uranium. It's radioactive, you know. That's why humanoids keep it under such strict lock and key in a laboratory."

"Okay. And that explains this… how, exactly?"

"We've been affected by carrying around this sample. It hasn't harmed us, at least I don't think, anyway. But now, it seems we have acquired some… telekinetic abilities."

"Meaning?"

"I think… when I asked you to grab that wrench, I made it come over to me. And when you started to panic, you caused the water pitcher to come over to us without meaning to."

Griffin leans back on a nearby countertop. "So, does that make us… special?"

Evander shrugs. "That's one way to put it, I guess."

"Are we okay to keep working on this?"

"I suppose, just be extra careful nothing important accidentally moves or breaks. After we finish working with it, I'd suggest we both head over to the infirmary to be treated for exposure. I wouldn't want my tools floating around like this for the rest of eternity."

"Really? I don't know, I think it's kind of cool."

"Cool? No, not really. Being a record keeper requires utmost knowledge of where everything is and how to get it. I can't be accidentally relocating important documents or tools, that would be a very bad thing. And don't tell anyone about it."

Griffin nods, and fiddles with his hair. "Okay, I suppose that makes sense. And, I think I'm ready."

"Good."

Over much of the next few Earth-equivalent hours, the mechanical genius and the tech prodigy work together to figure out the best placement of the uranium, as well as referring to the latest in inter-dimensional theories and past experiments. After a small eternity of hard work, Evander flips on a switch, and the entire, one-person time machine lights up in a myriad of rainbow colors. The subtle humming of the motor and the various lights sparkle in the relatively dim light of the record keeping office.

"I think... we did it."

***

"Luna, you did really well. I'm just wrapping up your wrist now. You can look now."

She turns her head to see that the doctor has covered her wrist with an almost jelly-like wrap, that seems to comfortably cool the affected area.

"This protective wrap is somewhat water proof, but also do your best to keep it as dry as possible - don't trust it too much. The stitches will dissolve on their own, but I'll expect you to come back in here after your next shift so I can check to make sure everything is healing properly. You'll be able to use your device once I activate it and take the wrapping off. Oh, and one more thing."

The doctor turns around to take a small bottle of pills off of a nearby table. "Here's some painkiller, in case it starts to hurt a bit once the sedative wears off."

Luna looks visibly concerned at his acknowledgment of possible pain that she might feel.

"There's no need to be concerned though, this was a very minor procedure. You'll be just fine, trust me."

Luna nods, and takes the small bottle from him. "How many, how often?"

"Take two every eight or so Earth hours." Luna nods, making a mental note to keep track by looking at the

Earth clock that is kept in the Sorting Room. Time moves a lot quicker on Earth than it does in the Upperworld, so Luna surmises that eight hours on Earth won't seem very long at all here.

"Take care, Luna. And remember, come see me after your next shift."

Luna nods, and heads back to her pod. She's feeling quite upset at Vidia for strong-arming her into this, but rules are rules, and as much as she does understand that, it is possible that the overly-zealous sorter may be a *bit* overbearing at times. Luna rolls her long sleeve over her operated wrist, and marvels at how comfortable the cooling wrap really is over the incision. But then she grimaces at the realization that the doctor gave her painkillers for a reason, and any comfort she feels now could wear off at any moment. She grits her teeth and continues walking, hoping to get her mind off of it.

On the way to her pod, she sees Evander and Griffin rolling some sort of large, mysterious object on a rolling cart toward the Grand Hall. Curious, but not wanting to seem too nosy, Luna puts off her nap a bit longer, and follows behind them without being detected.

CHAPTER 14

Onyx sits on his throne, as exhausted as ever. His hair and eyes are both glowing brighter and brighter every day. And more recently, his face has gotten more and more pale. He still manages to retain a bit of his natural pink complexion, but it looks to be on its way out. Onyx manages to sit up a little more and force a smile when he is met with the two Upperworld beings who might be able to set him free.

"Hello, Evander and Griffin. How's the time machine coming?" The two exchange knowing glances and then smile hesitantly at Onyx.

"Well, that's the thing…"

Onyx stiffens, waiting for them to announce some bad news.

"It's done."

"Seriously?" The glowing portions of his hair flare up, but only slightly. His fluorescent eyes glow a little brighter as well.

"Seriously! Now we came to talk to you because we're about ready to send someone to visit your mother. And since the machine appears to be only big enough to send one person, who are you most comfortable sending to retrieve the time coordinates?"

Onyx's mouth stands agape, trying to process all that they are saying about being ready to dig into his past. The thought of what they might find makes him feel more than a little uneasy and embarrassed, but it was necessary, and he knows that.

"It's up to you guys, I really don't have a preference." Evander and Griffin exchange confused glances.

"Really? Okay. So we'll post an ad and start interviewing candidates for..."

"Oh no, not that."

They both look back up to Onyx, who clears his throat. "I thought you meant between you two. It's gotta be one of you, and not just anyone. It's... sensitive information. I guess I do have that preference, at least."

Evander and Griffin look at each other, and then toward the machine. "Onyx, you should know that we really don't know what's on the other side of this. We think we'll be able to type in the year and geographic area, but beyond that, we aren't completely certain what would happen to the traveler."

"Yes and?" Onyx clearly isn't getting their point - usually, he'd be quite a bit more sympathetic than this. But right now, he is, understandably, very tired of being stuck on that throne.

"Well, uh, okay. I guess it's between us then." Evander turns to look at Griffin. They look at each other, and then back at Onyx, many times.

"I'll go." Both of them turn around to see Luna walking toward them down the long corridor of the Grand Hall. Onyx's hair burns even brighter, and his eyes seem to be ready to bore a hole in anything in their sight.

"Absolutely not!" Onyx doesn't bother with the pleasantries at this point.

"I can do it, Onyx. I'm stronger than ever, really." She approaches the throne, the same way she always has, and plants her feet solidly at its base.

"This is not up for debate, Luna. Time travel is even more risky than what you've done already. I'm not about to risk you getting hurt or... worse."

"But Onyx! I want to do something to help you! I hate sitting back, watching you suffer."

His eyes soften momentarily at her affections and bravery, but then brighten again. "Well be that as it may, I refuse to take that risk." He pauses. "Here's what I propose."

Griffin, Evander, and Luna all turn to look directly at Onyx, as his bright, shining blue eyes meet theirs.

"Griffin, I'd like you to be the one entering my past existence. Evander, as the more experienced one, I want you to monitor him to make sure he is okay and stays calm."

"What about me, Onyx?" Luna holds his gaze with the intensity of a thousand stars, awaiting his response with baited breath.

"Luna, for the first time ever, I don't want you involved in this at all. There's just no need, Evander and Griffin will handle it."

Both Griffin and Evander are stuck in silence, but they slowly nod their heads and prepare to put their plan into motion. Luna doesn't give up so easily.

"Onyx, why? I have more experience on Earth than they do. I can do this!"

"Just because you can, doesn't mean you should. Listen to me - if you want a life with me, off of this throne, you *cannot and will not jeopardize your own.* Do you understand me?"

Luna nods, with her fists at her side and her cheeks turning red with frustration.

"Griffin, are you prepared to go now? Is the machine ready?"

Both Evander and Griffin nod. "Yes, it appears to be ready to work."

"Excellent. Evander, I assume you know the time and place, right?"

"I do - Earth year 1790, New England area of the United States of America."

Onyx frowns. "You'll have to be more specific than that - did you seriously expect to drop him somewhere in that region and have him find my mother completely randomly? No, absolutely not. Figure out where to put him or I'll have to do it myself, and we both know I really don't have the energy for that kind of thing anymore."

Evander shuffles his feet nervously - he's not used to Onyx being this testy, but, then again, he supposes anyone would be if their butt was perpetually stuck to a chair draining the energy out of them as well. "I'll figure it out, don't worry about it." He then takes out his tablet and begins typing in his login credentials. "Oh I've got it -

She's in Massachusetts. Or, she *was* in Massachusetts... when she was alive."

Onyx grimaces at the thought of his own mother's death - or, at least, the mother he was supposed to have, had she not ended his life before it even had a chance to begin. He harbored many mixed feelings about the woman, ever since he had heard of her existence.

Evander begins going to work, inputting the information into the digitized screen that he recently installed onto it. He then hands the tracking / communication wristband to Griffin.

"Griffin, this wristband will allow me to track you on the screens in the record keeping office. Also, it will work as a back-up so that you can still talk to me even after your embedded device expels itself."

"After it does what now?"

Evander takes a deep breath, and steadies himself by placing a hand on Griffin's shoulder. "After twenty-four hours on Earth, your embedded device will expel itself from your body. DO not panic, and do not fight it. That is why you have the wristband. Needless to say, that wristband is your lifeline here. That's how you get back, once you tell me what the time coordinates of the turning point are. I cannot zap you back like the transport room can because this is a whole new venture entirely, and it is quite far out of the transport room's domain. I don't want to scare you or anything, but lose the bracelet, and it's game over. Understood?"

70

Griffin slowly nods, but is understandably apprehensive.

"I know you can do this."

They both turn around in response to Onyx's booming voice. Something about that throne must be amplifying him more than usual. "You can do this because I believe in you. Now, try to take confidence in that, okay? Oh, and when you see my *dear* mother... tell her to go -"

"Onyx! That's so rude..." Luna interrupts his vulgar suggestion, obviously mortified and surprised that he would allude to such a thing.

He rolls his eyes. "Well, killing isn't all that nice either, you know!" His attempt to lighten the mood has quite the opposite effect.

After strapping on the bracelet as tightly as it will go without cutting off circulation, Griffin hesitantly climbs into the time machine and locks the door behind him. After a few labored breaths, Evander hits the launch button on the machine. As it hums to life, the lights begin blinking erratically, until a bright blast of light makes everyone in the room cover their eyes. And then it is done. Evander gingerly opens the door, to find that Griffin is quite gone.

"It worked."

VOLUME TWO: CONSTANCE

CHAPTER 1

"Fae, ready yourself for school! We are both going to be late."

I pull on my own apron and head covering, and then pick up my rucksack from the kitchen table with the graded assignments from the children I teach at the schoolhouse.

"Constance, just a minute!" My younger sister emerges from our shared bedroom, as my mother enters the kitchen, holding our crying baby brother, Jedidiah.

"Good morning, mother." Our dual chorus elicits a calm smile from my mother's lips as she settles down onto the wooden bench Father built years ago when our family home was built.

"You are both going to be late - that is unacceptable, especially for a schoolmistress." Mother's bright blue, well-meaning eyes mirror my own, but double their intensity.

"I realize that, Mother, my apologies. We were just about to leave. Come along, Fae." I give Jedidiah a quick kiss on his soft little forehead, and then follow my younger sister out the door. We make the long trek through the compound, waving to our friends, the Abbotts, as we pass. I try to hide my smile as Finn's gaze lingers over me probably longer than it should. If the elders noticed, we'd be sternly spoken to. I shake off the slight blush emerging on my face, and follow my sister to the schoolhouse. We make it there just before the students enter the room, taking their places behind their assigned desks and pallets.

"Good morning students." I smile at them as they all file into to the small schoolhouse, and then I walk around opening as many windows as I can to let the warm sun in on this beautiful spring morning.

"Good morning, Mistress Miller."

"Today, we're going to work on our times tables. Who can tell me what five multiplied by seven equals?" Many hands shoot up into the air in excitement. The rest of the morning flies by quite quickly, so by the time I realize the students should be dismissed for lunch and recess, I barely notice my younger sister lingering at my desk.

"Is something the matter, Fae?"

She shakes her head in the negative, and I notice a small smirk form at the corner of her lips. She pushes some of her medium blonde hair out of her face, and then opens her mouth to speak.

"I heard Mother discussing something interesting yesterday."

"Oh?" I try to hide my amusement as I busy myself with clearing the chalkboard from our arithmetic lesson earlier. Usually Fae loves to share the latest gossip with me, as she's always been rather precocious despite her meager age of only twelve years old.

"Mother was speaking with Goody Brewster about some interesting matters."

"Such as what?" I finish wiping down the chalkboard, so I move toward my own lunch pail to open

74

the sandwich I had packed earlier. I waste no time in indulging in a generous mouthful of mother's homemade roast beef and garden-grown lettuce and tomatoes.

"Such as you."

"Me?" My interest is piqued at this point, but I continue eating nonchalantly.

"Yes you. She finds you to be a favorable match for Silas."

And that's precisely when the roast beef bits fly out of my mouth and onto my otherwise pristinely-kept desk.

"Silas? Me?"

Fae nods excitedly. "Isn't that fantastic! Silas is so nice and friendly…"

She seems thrilled on my behalf, but truth be told, I still can't quite swallow either the news she divulged or the bit of sandwich caught in my throat. I start to sputter, and quickly reach for my water jug. I douse my throat with the lukewarm liquid, and then try to process what my sister said to me.

"Honestly, Fae. I'm not… interested in Silas. I never really have been." My mind wastes no time conjuring the latest image of Silas from last week's church fellowship, and all I can see is the rotund, fatty portion of his protruding gut that seems to threaten to bust his clothing at the seams. He always chews with his mouth wide open and is utterly disgusting - but I elect to leave out those insensitive details for my sister's sake.

Fae's smile rapidly fades, and then her eyes widen. "Oh. I wasn't aware it'd make you unhappy. I'm sorry,

Constance. I should have had the foresight to keep it to myself. That is, if I heard her correctly. I might be wrong. I hope, for your sake, that I misheard their intent."

I force a smile and pat her gently on the shoulder. "Don't you worry about me, I'll be all right, God willing." In our family, and many others like it, 'God willing' is a largely overused term, but it suffices to fill in any gaps in conversation that are otherwise left unfilled.

"Okay. Sorry, again, about that." My sister sadly walks out the door of the schoolhouse to join her friends on the school grounds. I'm left alone with my half-eaten sandwich and the partially-chewed bits of it that landed on my desk. As I fetch a nearby rag to clean up the mess, I can't shake the dull aching that I feel in the pit of my stomach. Somehow, I have a bad feeling that I'm going to find out what she meant very, very soon.

✳✳✳

"Griffin. Are you there? Come in, Griffin."

He materialized only moments ago, and finds himself on a grassy area near a schoolhouse.

"I'm here, I think I made it. What year is it, again?"

He hears whooping and hollering on the other side of the receiver built into his bracelet, and once they settle down long enough to respond to him, he hears Evander on the other end answer him. "Griffin, you are in Earth year

1790. Congratulations! We did it, you are the first time traveler ever!"

Griffin steps back, leaning against the tree behind him. "Wow. Okay. That's... incredible."

"Don't celebrate too much yet though. We've got to get you back safe before we get too thrilled. Okay. I'm going to try to guide you to Constance."

"Who?"

"That's his mother. Onyx's mother, that is."

Griffin sharply exhales, and waits for further instructions. "Okay, what do I do? Where is she, how do I recognize her?"

Evander hesitates to answer him, as he's not totally sure, but then consults the top-secret files on his tablet. "Okay, so it seems that she was a schoolteacher, and looks to have blonde hair and bright blue eyes... Just like Onyx."

Griffin nods. "What is a 'schoolteacher'?"

"Well, on Earth, older humanoids teach the younger humanoids basic skills to help them in life and to provide a certain level of prestige."

"Oh, okay." Griffin nods, even though he quickly realizes that no one can see him. "So where is she, exactly?"

"Don't know for sure, but maybe checking the schoolhouse in front of you would be a good place to start." Evander's sass is unmistakable, even through the receiver.

"Right, okay. Will do."

"But Griffin, you *must* be extremely cautious about two things. One - she cannot find you, because you might change the course of history. Stay in hiding. Two - don't talk to anyone, if you can help it. I understand you may need to procure food, and other necessities, but do so very carefully. This is unprecedented, and as I've established, we don't actually know how time travel is going to affect things. Be aware of that and tread lightly."

"I understand, Evander. I will do my best. Remind me again, what exactly I am watching her for?"

"You need to find the precise moment when she decides to abort the baby. We've placed you there about a week before its conception. Watch her, and tell us the specific time coordinates of her decision."

"Time coordinates?"

"On your wristband, there is a small screen with numbers moving every second, correct? I need you to look at that and tell me what it says at that moment. There is a bit of wiggle room if it is slightly off, but get it as close as you can. I can play around with slight variations if I need to."

"I'm on it. Sit tight, I'll let you know."

CHAPTER 2

When school is dismissed for the day, I pack up my things, and wait for Fae to be ready so I can walk home with her. I close the door behind me and walk at a leisurely pace while she skips next to me, clanking her lunch pail against a nearby wooden fence.

"Constance, when is the spelling test again? I always forget."

I fight the urge to roll my eyes, and give her a stern glance instead. "Next Thursday. I do hope you've been studying. It's on list eighteen - did you leave your text at school again?"

Fae sheepishly nods.

"Well, it's no matter. You can get it tomorrow - you won't need it tonight anyway." I continue walking toward our house as Fae skips a bit ahead of me, but it's just as well, because we pass the Abbott home again. And I happen to see Finn working the field with his pa. His white shirt is soaked almost completely through with sweat, and he undoes a few of the lacings to let his strong chest get some of the fresh spring air.

"Constance, you're *staring...*"

Fae must have turned back and caught up with me, because she's inches from my ear and clearly embarrassed on my behalf. I wish I could say I was, but I was mesmerized. It's hard to say exactly what about him was doing that to me.

I've known him since I was in primary school myself - years before I began teaching. I remember he used to throw little bits of white chalk at the back of my head, and I would always turn around and scowl at him. I used to be so utterly annoyed at him... that is, until I wasn't anymore.

"Come on, let's go. Ma's probably fixing dinner by now." Fae pulls at my hand, but I might as well be stuck in a puddle of molasses. Not even caring how odd I look, I stand in place as Finn sees me and immediately walks over to the road from his yardwork. The sweat on his face and body glistens in the sun, and I tell myself not to stare too obviously.

"Hello there, *Mistress* Miller. Lovely day, isn't it?" He elongates my title of respect, as if to make fun of me or to honor me. I'm not totally sure which, it seems ambiguity in this case was what he was striving for.

"Good day, Finn." I can feel my face heating up, and I just hope it's not too noticeable. It's not good to be so obviously smitten in a public place.

"And how was school for you, Fae?" He smiles sweetly at my younger sister, who just shrugs and starts fiddling with the knot on her apron.

"It was fine, I suppose."

Finn feigns shock and covers his mouth with a grimy hand from working a long day in the field that wasn't quite over yet. "Fine? But your dear sister is your teacher, is she not? You should be more grateful to her for teaching you so well."

80

Fae pouts, clearly embarrassed, but she's unable to articulate an appropriate response.

"Aw, don't worry. There's fresh squeezed lemonade in the kitchen if you want a glass. Go ask my ma for some."

"Finn, we really should be going..." But Fae is already halfway to the front door of the Abbott home. As tired as I was already, I take a step forward to chase after her, but a strong, yet gentle hand on my arm holds me back. I try to ignore the warmth spreading to my entire body from his touch on my wrist.

"Constance, I just wanted to say... you looked beautiful today. This morning, I saw you and just... I had to say it."

I meet his deep brown eyes with my bright blue ones, and I try to say something equally respectable and intelligent, but nothing more than some hesitant mumbling escapes my lips. I blush even redder, embarrassed at my own inaptitude.

"No need to respond, I can see that I must have inhibited your ability to speak." He smirks at me, fully reading my much-too-obvious body language, to my chagrin.

"Well, I, uh..." I look over to the open door to catch a glimpse of Fae chatting pleasantly with Goody Abbott. "Thank you very much, for the lemonade, Goody, but Fae and I really must be going."

She nods happily, and places the pitcher of lemonade back onto the tabletop. "Always a pleasure, girls. God be with ye."

I smile back and grab Fae's slightly sticky hand from the lemonade condensation. "Goodbye, *Master* Abbott." I take a great amount of pleasure beating him at his own game, as recognition hits his face and he smirks, clearly noticing my slick reaction to his earlier joke.

Fae and I continue the walk back to our house, waving to other neighbors as we pass by. But none of them catch my eye nearly as much as Finn.

✳✳✳

"Onyx, do you want to see your mother?" Evander approaches Onyx's throne hesitantly, as he has noticed Onyx become more easily agitated as of late.

"What do you mean?" The remaining color drains out of Onyx's face, even though there isn't much left to speak of at this point.

"Your mother. We're tracking her through Griffin. You can see the footage, if you want. I think you've got her eyes." Evander smiles at him, but Onyx appears unable to respond. After much silence, Onyx nods slowly.

"All right, I suppose I'll see her." He audibly swallows, and sits up straighter in his seat-turned-prison.

Evander smiles at Luna, who is also sitting nearby. With a few clicks of his tablet, Evander projects the most recent footage of Constance onto the large screen of the Grand Hall.

At the sight of her walking with another, younger girl on a bustling street corner, his face seems to soften momentarily before it hardens again. His lips, which seemed to be fighting an almost-smile, move back into their more customarily neutral position.

"See? I told you she has your eyes."

"His hair too - she's very blonde..." Luna chimes in happily, momentarily oblivious to his discomfort.

Onyx remains silent, and begins tapping his fingertips incessantly on the armrest of his throne.

"Maybe so, but she never gave herself a chance to see them."

Evander and Luna exchange troubled glances, but they quickly compose themselves long enough to keep Onyx from getting too upset.

"Well, I guess it just wasn't meant to be, then." Luna tries to smile at him thoughtfully to diffuse some of the pain she imagines that he probably feels, but to no avail.

"Luna, it's more complicated than that... and you know it." His eyes begin to glow an even brighter blue as his flaming hair seems to grow even stronger. She nods in response, but her own violet eyes fail to hide the strongest of emotion she feels - that of longing. He longs for what never was, and Luna longs for what once was and is no longer. Reconciling it all is what Griffin set out to do, but it is certainly easier said than done.

CHAPTER 3

"Good evening, Constance. How was your day?" Mother smiles at me from behind her favorite spot in the kitchen, seemingly preparing for our evening meal. Soft tendrils of her hair stick to her clammy forehead on this warm spring late afternoon.

"It was fine, Ma. Just another day." I move toward my bedroom in our small house - well, the one I share with Fae.

"Constance, where has Fae gone to? It is nearly time for supper. Your father will be home from the field any moment now." She looks curiously around the main room of our modest little home.

"She stopped to pick some of the flowers we passed on our way home, so she should be back any minute." Mother nods, and then looks down at the large blob of dough that she's kneading.

"Well, since I have you here alone for a moment, I suppose there's something we should discuss." My ears burn at the likely implication of her words - I can only imagine what it is she likely wants to talk to me about. And I'm not happy at the prospect as I am imagining it. She opens her mouth to continue speaking, but pauses. "How silly of me - I think we should wait until your father arrives home. I'm sure he would like to be a part of the conversation."

I nod as politely as I can manage, even though I catch myself tightly gripping a handful of my apron in my

84

right fist. I continue on toward my room just as Fae breezes through the front door.

"Fae! I told you to stay with your sister. Why did you dawdle like this?" Mother has her flour-covered hands on her hips, but I cannot mistake the smile tugging at the corners of her mouth as Fae sheepishly holds the makeshift bouquet fabricated from the wildflowers that grow along the side of the road.

"They're for you, Mother. I thought maybe you'd like them for the dinner table." Mother softens in response, and happily takes the flowers from Fae and deposits them in a pitcher of water.

"How thoughtful of you! They're very pretty, Fae. But do try to walk with your sister to and from school please. I don't want the rambunctious Johnson children to bother you again."

I roll my eyes at the thought of the family living a mere three houses away from ours, and the way that they always seemed to get their grubby fingers into everything - and I mean everything. They always seem to create and attract gossip like flies to honey, and there was no shortness of excitement when they are around - but not necessarily the good kind. There are four of them: Grace, Love, Calm, and Noble - and they couldn't be more ironically named. Noble, the eldest brother, who is a very immature twelve-year-old, always enjoys bothering Fae. At church last week, he was pulling her braids the entire time and refused to stop. I tried to swat him away without making a scene, but there just wasn't much I could do about it. I have a hunch that he fancies Fae, but she would be mortified at that prospect - and who could blame her? Calm, his younger and quite rambunctious brother is about ten years old, I believe and he is anything but. Just last month he was harshly punished for climbing on my father's horse without his permission - and nearly got kicked in the throat. Frankly, I think that would have served him right - the little maggot. Love and Grace are the eight-year old identical twins, and they enjoy pretending to be each other to confuse the entire compound. I still to this day am not completely sure which of them is which. Regardless of who is who, I can understand why Mother likely desires to keep Fae away from them at all costs - those children are nothing but bad news, and quite insufferable, if I do say so myself. Their parents do very little to inhibit them in their obnoxious escapades, much to everyone's dismay.

Fae nods her head, her braids bobbing energetically next to her ears. "Yes, Mother."

"Both of you, go wash your faces before dinner. It will be ready very shortly." We both grab our things and drop them off in our shared room before heading off to the washroom. After pouring some fresh, clean water into the basin, we both wash our faces and pat them dry with the hand-sewn face cloths that Mother made for each of us last summer. Emerging from the washroom, we take our places at the table, where Mother has prepared a lovely spread of fresh berry preserves with her homemade bread and butter, some roasted chicken from the butcher, and some fresh herbs and spices from our garden to season it with. The tomatoes are starting to sprout this time of year, but they won't be ripe for a while yet. She places a pitcher of water on the table, with another small jug of milk next to it - freshly gleaned from Bessie the cow this afternoon. I've always looked up to my mother, and the way that she always managed to put together a positively lovely meal no matter what was in season at the time.

I'm about to reach for the jug of milk when Father emerges from the doorway in an obvious huff. His shoulders are squared upon his back as his hands are jammed firmly into his pockets.

"Welcome home, Ezekial. Everything all right?" Mother gives him a chaste kiss on the cheek as Fae winces. Father nods his head but still appears displeased.

"I'm just fine, Hopestill. Just another day in the field with a bum knee, is all." He rubs his left knee gingerly, as he tries to nurse the injury from a couple months ago that still has not completely healed.

"I'll get you some hemp root for the pain. Children, please settle yourselves at the table." Mother disappears behind the curtain separating our home stash of apothecary goods, and emerged with a small jar with a brownish-green scrub in it. "This should help ease the pain. Here you are." Mother stoops down to gently roll up my father's left pant leg to apply the healing balm.

"Oh, that is wonderful. Thank you, my love." Father smiles at Mother as she stands back up, straightens her bonnet, and sits back down at her place setting.

"I was hoping it would work - and I'm so glad that it did. I had gone to ask Rafaela about it, and she made a special blend, just for you."

Father smiles, but seems to withhold any outright praise. "She may be talented at her work, but she is still quite... eccentric." He wrinkles his nose, and then reaches for the plate of chicken that Mother had prepared, but she quickly swats his hand away.

"We have yet to thank the Lord for the meal, Ezekial..." She quickly folds her hands and bows her head, as the rest of us follow suit. Father clears his throat loudly and then says our grace.

"Dear Lord, we thank you greatly for this bountiful meal, and for protection as we all went about our daily tasks. Please bless us as we partake in this nourishment, and grant us strength and diligence in all that we try to accomplish. In Your holy name, Amen."

Our echoes of "Amen" fill the main room of our house, and then we all reach for the food, this time without being swatted away by Mother. She exchanges a brief knowing glance with Father as Fae and I unceremoniously fill our mouths with food. Even baby Jedidiah seems to be quite enamored with the relatively unappetizing mush of tender chicken and fresh fruit that Mother laid out in front of him.

"Constance, there is a matter that involves you that your mother and I wish to speak to you about."

Oh goodness, not here, not now!

✳✳✳

"I followed her home, she appears to be eating a meal with her family at the moment." Griffin speaks quietly into his communicator as quietly as possible.

"Excellent. Keep watching. There really is no real way to be sure about *the moment*, but I have every confidence in you that you'll know when you see it." Evander's voice replies back to him at an equally quiet volume - yet another safety feature that Evander managed to install to retain as much secrecy as possible. "Also, do make sure you are not detected by anyone. If you are hungry, there are ample gardens around that you may be able to pick from. And based on your geographical location, there are many haystacks around - that should be suitable coverage and a comfortable place to sleep for you."

Griffin awkwardly nods, and then becomes painfully aware that Evander cannot see his every move - only what is available from the monitor in the Grand Hall. "Affirmative - I will take care of myself the best I can without arousing any concern from the humanoids."

"Exactly. That is indeed the best course of action at this time. The moment we are looking for is still quite a ways away, I believe, as she is only being made aware of her parent's plans as we speak. You are more than welcome to, quite literally, hit the hay for the night if you'd prefer. You must be quite tired from your miraculous journey through time!"

"Indeed, I feel quite exhausted for sure. Thank you for your help, Evander. I will see you soon, I surely do hope." He ends the call on his wrist device and stealthily moves toward a nearby garden to pluck some not-quite-ripe tomatoes off of a vine. Sinking his teeth into the hard skin and the still-bitter juice of the fruit, he spits it out and begins looking for a suitable alternative. Finding a loaf of bread on the ground, he can barely believe his luck as he grabs it and begins consuming it voraciously. What he doesn't see, is the small child who dropped it there for him.

CHAPTER 4

Onyx's tears begin rolling down his face even before Evander notices and clicks off the live feed signal from Griffin's transmitter. Shifting his weight awkwardly, he waits until Onyx composes himself to comment.

"Are you... okay?"

Onyx meets his gaze intensely, seeming to be both having a lot to say and wanting to say nothing at all. "I will be...just fine, Evander. I've just... never laid eyes on her before. Seeing her face... and her family... my family. It's... a lot to process."

Evander looks over to where Luna is seated near his throne, and notices the subtle glint of tears forming at the corner of her eyes as well. "I hate seeing him suffer like this. And I hate seeing you suffer like this too."

Luna shrugs in response to Evander, and he continues waiting for Onyx to comment further on what they have just seen.

"Don't worry about me, I'll be fine." Onyx's hair glows, and then dims, a vestige of living color spreading onto the rest of his being and the surrounding walls of the Grand Hall as well.

"Luna, look at me." Luna lifts her head in his general direction, but hesitates to meet his gaze. "No, I mean *really* look at me. Please?" His tone softens as he senses her pain, and forces himself to smile even amidst his own discomfort.

"I'm trying, I just wish… none of this happened. I wish… you were allowed to live. I wish, *we* were…"

Onyx nods, understanding her all too well, as Evander respectfully looks away. "I'll give you two a moment." He collects his equipment and then leaves the large room momentarily.

"Would it have mattered?"

Onyx pauses. "Would what have mattered, Luna?"

She swallows before clarifying her thought. "Would it have mattered… if we both lived? Why weren't we allowed to?"

He sighs. "Earth is very, very twisted in that way. Unfortunately, the arrival of a child is not always met with joy and excitement. Sometimes - many times, such news is extremely inconvenient and problematic, to put it moderately."

"How so? I was… just a person. How much could have gone wrong?"

Onyx rests his face in his hands, and continues to sob through his words. "Luna, I can assure you, if you had studied anthropology on Earth the way I have, you'd understand. Humanoids are vastly complex creatures with more subtle nuances and caveats than any document or digital system in the Upperworld. Many times, cultural and religious expectations play a large role in their expectations. I have a hunch… that's exactly what happened here. With my mother. And then, as a result, with you.

***

"We've found you a suitor."

I nearly choke on the bite of food I just placed in my mouth. "Excuse me?"

Both Father and Mother nod excitedly. "Indeed - Silas Brewster. Isn't that quite wonderful? The Brewster clan has held great wealth and power through their iron smith business, and have upheld wonderful reputations amongst everyone they know. This will bring glory to both families in the eyes of God, as well as ensure a proper future for you - which wouldn't include useless hours teaching at the school house, I might add."

Matching smiles spread across their faces while my own face feels utterly paralyzed in shock and dread. Fae looks equally upset on my behalf, but also remains silent. Baby Jedidah just continues nibbling contentedly on a piece of bread.

"Mother, Father?"

They smile at me, hanging on my every word. "I don't fancy Silas." I wait for their reaction, and brace myself for the impact. They exchange troubled glances as I refrain from saying anything more.

"What exactly do you mean, you don't *fancy* Silas?" Father's frown is accompanied by a furrowed brow, and he taps his fingers on our oak-topped kitchen table perpetually. The tapping mimics the pounding of my heart and suddenly the silence in my head feels much louder than the words that we are likely to share between us. I gulp, waiting for my thoughts to take shape in a way that wouldn't positively throw my home life into utter turmoil.

"Father, I do not want to be betrothed to Silas." I close my jaw in a calm defiance, fighting the urge to run out of the room and cry. At least not yet, anyway.

"Constance, I am greatly saddened to hear of your discordant feelings surrounding the matter. I truly did want you to be happy about the arrangement."

I release some of the tension in my shoulders. Father seems to be hearing me out, maybe he'll understand. Maybe I won't be stuck with that fat pig forever. Maybe I have hope.

"Unfortunately, the binding promises have already been made. I sold them three cows to pay your dowry."

My breath catches in my throat. "What? But Father, that's not... I can't. Surely you can suggest some kind of reparations to be made? Father, please..." I begin whimpering as the tears quit threatening to fall down my cheeks and end up parading down them against my will. My voice wavers, and my whole body shivers. I'm not sure if it's anger, or fear. Probably both.

"Constance, my hands are tied. You are betrothed to Silas Brewster, and you shall marry in about two week's time."

I am shocked silent, and I feel absolutely sick at this news. I grasp for anything to at least delay the inevitable. "But Father, the schoolhouse - I haven't found my replacement yet. The students will need to be taught until my replacement is found."

Father nods. "I am quite aware of that fact, which is why I asked your mother to ask around on your behalf. It appears that the Smith family has a daughter just a year or two younger than you, and she is quite equipped for the job. You don't need to concern yourself with that anymore. You will say goodbye to the schoolchildren by the end of next week."

I look at Mother with desperate eyes, but she seems unable to meet my gaze. Suddenly the spice rack next to the hearth appears to hold more importance than her agonizing daughter. Without seeing a way out, I excuse myself from the table and retire to my room for the evening.

"I'm suddenly not very hungry."

CHAPTER 5

Griffin is eating the loaf of bread quite loudly as the fluffy dough satisfies his hunger. As he is about halfway through the loaf, he feels the uncanny sensation that he is being watched, so he looks up from the bread in the direction that he can feel it from. And sure enough, he is met with a pair of very young, brown eyes fixated on his very noticeable, light-blue suited form.

"Hello. I'll just be going now." Griffin inches as far away as he can possibly get, around the corner of the building he was standing near. But the child follows him. He looks to be around maybe ten years old, and is dressed similarly to the other humanoids, in some form of work clothes, most likely.

"Who are you?" His voice hits Griffin's ears like the foreboding sound of a hurricane in the distance.

"I'm, well, nobody. I'm just passing through. Goodbye."

"Hey Nobody, you're dressed different. Why?"

Griffin turns back around slowly, and then looks down at his own clothing in comparison to that of the child's. "It's just my style. No reason." He turns around to walk away with his bread, and is relieved to hear silence in his wake. That is, until the child grabs onto his ankle and prevents him from leaving.

"That is my foot. I have no business here, so I am leaving. Please let go." Griffin tries his best to shake him off, but to no avail. The child appears to be stuck on his ankle as securely as the jaws of life.

"I'm not letting go until you tell me who you are, Nobody." The brown eyes glare at him from their lower vantage point, boring into his own eyes.

"Okay, then I'll tell you who I am." Griffin pauses just long enough to think of a suitable answer. "I'm a helper. Who was sent here. To do important work. All right? Now *get off*." Griffin isn't normally combative, but in this moment, he feels he has no other choice than to be a little tougher.

"Not until you tell me who you are helping, and why."

"That wasn't the agreement though!" Griffin is becoming visibly upset now, as his fists are clenching and unclenching at his sides, one if them still holding the half-eaten piece of bread.

"Calm! It's time for supper. Come home!" Griffin looks across the street to see a woman standing outside the front door of her home, glancing toward the child anchored on his leg. She stands as defiantly as her child is trapping him. "I'm serious Calm, the stew is getting cold! Come along now." She taps her foot in frustration. "Who is that over there? Calm?" Griffin sees her walking down the three steps from their small front porch and marching toward her child. If she gets too close to Griffin, he knows he's a goner. Or the entire historical narrative may be, if it wasn't already. With a sudden burst of well-timed energy, he manages to break free while the child is distracted, and make a break for the nearby field. Their conversation floats near his ears as he makes a hasty getaway.

"Calm! Who was that peculiar man?"

"I dunno, Ma. He just said he was Nobody. And some sort of a helper."

✳✳✳

"Onyx, it seems Griffin has been spotted by a couple of humanoids."

His flaming hair glows the brightest it's ever been, as he winces from the burning sensation it produces.

"What? How? Did you not tell him to be careful about that? He could throw everything off!" Onyx appears visibly ill-at-ease, and for good reason. Time travel is so unwieldy, and even the slightest change in any moment could ruin human history as a whole. And oftentimes, it could happen when it is least expected.

"I absolutely did, I can assure you of that." Evander rubs his hand through his hair. "It's just... unpredictable. He can only be so careful, some things are out of his control."

Onyx nods, but still appears upset. "It's just scary is all. How many possible variables there are. How completely and utterly foggy the concept of existence is. It's enough to boggle the mind ten times over.."

Evander looks at Luna next to him, and then they both shift their glances back to Onyx. "Well, I suppose that's true. I just always followed the rules, never gave it any real thought beyond that."

Luna nods in agreement. "Me too, Onyx. I always just did exactly what you told me to, you know? I never thought much of it. I also never really believed there was much I could do to really change anything at all."

Onyx strokes the pale skin of his chin while thinking about the ideas and words flowing between the two people in existence that he has the strongest emotional ties with. "Do you believe in the alternate universe theories?"

"I'm not sure, it's... highly theoretical. Just as theoretical as time travel, I'd say." Evander scratches the back of his own neck.

"Well, we managed to figure out time travel, so it just goes to show you that nothing is impossible, really." Luna pipes in, with the interest visibly sparkling in her violet eyes.

"It's just something I've always wondered about. The idea that there are other realities in infinite numbers, just like this one... it's riveting."

Luna nods. "But, is that actually important for anything right now? I don't really see a use for that like we did for time travel."

"I suppose you're right... but it doesn't hurt to be aware of such possibilities. Maybe such thoughts can free us from the traps we have set for ourselves. We are always so terrified of changing the course of human history. But, why are we, really? Does it matter if things change from the way they were intended? Is the evolution of the grand narrative really that bad?" His blue eyes glow brighter and brighter as the thoughts take hold in his head.

"Onyx, not to rain on your parade but… there's so much more to it than that. Human lives exist in and around each other. If the story changes, then people that would have been born may not be. And drastic changes like that have massive ripple effect potential. The entire Upperworld was thrown into an absolute frenzy when an orb was sorted incorrectly. Surely you wouldn't wish that to happen again."

The glow dims from his eyes, and Luna slumps back into her chair.

CHAPTER 6

I stay in my bedroom for the rest of the night. I just needed time. Time to think, time to process everything. I'm not shocked that this is happening, but I hate that I'm being forced. It makes my entire body shake with an anger I didn't know I would be capable of possessing.

Since I was about maybe six or seven years old, my parents have raised me with the full knowledge that I would be given away to a boy at some point. I was never given an exact time frame, though. And I absolutely wasn't expecting it now - after all, I only just turned sixteen a few weeks ago. Well, then again, that may have just been because I was living in denial. A couple of my friends were already married - Hope was betrothed and married to Humility Wilson last year. They were nervous about it at first, but they ended up loving each other, so I convinced myself it was a cute enough story. But now I know I was just trying to give myself a chance at a brighter future than what I was given.

I wanted more than just being a housewife. I loved drawing, even though mother tells me that's far too vain. I keep a sketchbook and pencils under my bed and draw in my spare time. I've been told by my students that I'm pretty good at it, and over time, I started to believe them. Then my imagination really took over, and I began to think that maybe I might be able to be a famous artist someday. It's frivolous, I know. Silly, even. But I can't shake the feeling that a marriage right now would mean the death of that dream. And I am absolutely sure, without a shadow of doubt, that marrying Silas would kill every bit of myself. Letting a dream die is hard enough, but marrying that boy, I knew, would relegate me to a mere shell of what I once was. That is, implying that I ever was anything notably important - which sometimes, I felt that I wasn't.

There have been days when I have absolutely loved everything about my family and life. I loved Fae and baby Jedidiah, of course. But our parents are so misguided - just like the rest of the compound. Everyone here is so bizarre. I've heard of people in other parts of the world who married for love. And the rich and wealthy waited until they were a bit older as well. How monstrous of a misfortune it is to have to hurry life along at the pace of a rabbit's heart beat, with a fat, ugly, blob-like betrothed who wanted nothing but warm meals and what lies below my waistband. It's disgusting, all of it.

I awoke early this morning, screaming into my pillow, attempting to muffle the sound enough to avoid waking my family. A quick look out my window reaffirms what I assumed to be true, that my whirling thoughts and anxiety of my impending psychological death continue to exist and weren't merely a bad dream. The morning was about to dawn, but by my approximations, it would be a little while before the Saturday morning chores were expected to begin. On non-school days, I had the luxury of a slightly later start to my day. And today, I knew just who I needed to talk to.

Tiptoeing around my room, I quietly dress myself, pulling on my undergarments, petticoat and apron. As early as the hour is, I opt to leave my head covering on its hook, as a subtle act of defiance. Besides, I knew who I was going to visit, and she definitely would not mind that my head was left uncovered. And given my plight as of late, I know she'll know just what to say to make it better, somehow.

I open the front door of our home, wincing as the creaky door makes itself known. Mother has been reminding Father to grease that for ages, but he's been far too busy with the spring planting. I smile to myself as I manage to close the door behind me without any frustrated footsteps following it, and then make my way down the sleepy street as people are beginning to start their day in the wee hours of the morning before the sun rises.

The deep purplish sky over my head shows the passing of time, and I make a mental note to be back at home before the sun completely rises. I fully enjoy the fresh, crisp feeling of the spring morning air on my scalp, and I allow myself to gratuitously undo the tight braids that I slept in. Shaking my long light-blonde hair free of itself, I can't help but smile at the way I feel so free. That's quite ironic, of course, given the circumstances. But true, all the same.

The leather soles of my homemade shoes hit the stone-covered pathway into town, where I knew Rafaela would be setting up her apothecary shop for the market today. She only rolls into the compound on the weekends, but I always made an effort to see her when I could. Since she doesn't live here, and seems to live under her own terms instead of terms imposed upon her, I've always seen her as kind of a role model. I'd break out of this compound if I could and run far, far away. But I have no place to go, and the realist in me knows all too well that those ideas are far better left as unfulfilled daydreams.

I nod politely at the few people that I pass by who likely had the same idea I did about enjoying the fresh morning air. Some of them wave and smile, like Goody Abbott as I pass by Finn's house. I wave and smile back, always finding her relaxed mindset and progressive attitude refreshing in contrast with my more legalistic family and their suffocatingly traditionalist values. I try not to look for Finn's attractive silhouette in the window that I know leads to his bedroom, but in the dim light of dawn, I can just manage to see his chiseled frame as he pulls on his working shirt. I thank my lucky stars that his mother seems not to have noticed, and I continue my walk into the marketplace. I make a mental note to move a bit faster in order to afford myself a few minutes to chat with Rafaela and have time to make the trek back home before my absence is noticed.

As my feet start to become tired from the elevated pace I forced them into, I sigh in relief as Rafaela's apothecary stand comes into view. I smile at the cheery dark blue lettering that she likely painted herself from blueberry pigment. She's always been so creative and talented, as long as I've known her.

"Good morning, Rafaela!" I jog over to her and smile. She turns to me and gives me a big hug as her long, dark hair falls over my shoulder. I meet her orchid-colored irises.

"Dearest Constance! How have you been, my dear?" She pulls me close for a moment, and then takes a good, long look at me.

"I'm... all right, mostly. Happy to see you, anyway!"

She nods excitedly, her ornate jewelry bobbing around her face and neck. I notice the decadent texture of her colorful dress, and can't help but envy the freedom of movement that the thin fabric likely also affords.

"No head covering today? How lovely to see such pretty hair!" Her laugh tickles my ears and I smile as the sound reverberates through my skull.

"I just needed some fresh air this morning. It's been far too long since I've seen you last!"

Rafaela nods. "Indeed, my friend. I've been busy traveling around to some other places, but I'm hoping to be around in this region for the spring season, at least. It's so beautiful here this time of year."

I smile at her in response, but even that smile fades quicker than I can maintain it. "There is... something that I just found out about yesterday."

"Oh?" Her rose-painted lips make a soft "o" as she places small vials onto her display holder and straightens a bowl of healing stones sitting nearby.

"My family, you see, they've arranged a marriage for me."

Rafaela blinks. "And is that not cause for congratulations?" She brushes a few strands of her jet-black hair out of her eyes.

"Typically, it might be. But the boy they have arranged for me... I don't fancy him at all."

Rafaela frowns, and then pats me on the shoulder. "That is certainly difficult. But you should know that I have heard of many people who have learned to love their arrangement over time. Maybe you will too?" She tries to smile at me, but I can't return it, and I can see the pain pulling down the corners of her mouth too.

"Not this one, Rafaela. There's..." I pause, looking around me to make sure there aren't any potential listeners in earshot. ".... someone *else* that I fancy."

Her frown deepens, and I watch as her shoulders deflate like a balloon. She opens her mouth to speak, but cannot seem to get the words out. I allow myself to succumb to her embrace, as she pulls me close, even tighter than before.

"My poor dear..." Her words, even though she appears to be just a handful of years older than me, hold a certain amount of weight and wisdom to them that I cannot place exactly, but I believe them all the same.

CHAPTER 7

Griffin awakens early from his slumber in the field he had escaped to the other evening when the small child had latched himself to his leg and refused to let go. The prickly yet soft texture of the grass brought awareness and wakefulness to the back of his neck and fingertips, and he manages to sit up, albeit a bit more slowly due to the different gravity level he is still adapting to.

Before he manages to come to his full standing height, an abrupt and uncomfortable almost choking sensation makes itself known to his throat. He remembers the bread that he ate last night, and suddenly worries he has been poisoned. Struggling to tap into his remote communicator from the time machine, he begins to cough and sputter nearly uncontrollably.

"Evander! I can't… breathe. Something is… hurting me…"

"Griffin! Stay calm. Can you describe what you feel?"

"My throat… something is… fighting to get out."

A few moments tick by as Griffin is met with silence on the other end of the communicator. "Griffin, you do not need to panic. I am relatively certain that your embedded device is just being expelled."

"My what?"

"Yes, that's exactly why we made sure you had a secondary communication device that you could keep with you even after it was expelled. Remember we talked about the safety feature that is imprinted in your embedded device? Twenty-four hours on Earth, and it makes its own hasty exit."

"Oh, that." His speech is cut out by some more coughing as the device rapidly makes its way up his esophagus. "I didn't realize. I thought... I thought I was... poisoned."

"That is quite unlikely, at least from what you are describing. You are just fine, Griffin. But I can stay online with you, if that helps. At least until it's out."

Griffin nods, and then gives a verbal affirmative since Evander obviously can't see him.

"It's almost, oh... it's... spindly."

"Those were the wires previously attached to your nervous system. You don't need to worry about it now - it's virtually useless at this point. You'll get it replaced as soon as you return to the Upperworld."

"Thank you, Evander. Oh, and I should tell you, I sort of, accidentally, got into a bit of a squabble with a young humanoid, I really didn't mean to -"

"I know, Griffin, we saw the whole thing from our monitor up here."

"Oh." The embarrassment and feeling of failure in his voice is palpable. "I hope everything's still all right. I know that's risky business."

"It is, but everything seems okay at the moment. Just be careful, please."

"Absolutely. I won't let you down." Griffin fingers the odd, black, spindly, creature-like mechanism that he coughed up, almost forgetting that it used to live comfortably under the surface of his skin on his wrist.

"On behalf of the Upperworld and every human who lives now and will live in the future, I surely hope so."

✳✳✳

"What was that about?" Evander turns around to meet Luna's inquisitive eyes.

"Oh, Griffin. His embedded device ejected itself and he didn't know what was going on. I could have sworn we warned him about that. Regardless, he was pretty concerned until I allayed some of his fears."

"That is pretty scary. I remember when I lost mine - I didn't expect it either."

"Yeah it definitely feels odd. At least, I imagine it would."

"I was in a store on Earth when it happened. I was almost choking on the device when it was trying to leave my body."

Evander nods. "Glad you made it back here as safely as you did."

"I'm glad I wasn't alone... the whole time anyway."

Onyx jumps in to the conversation from his vantage point on the throne. "Because I was there with you?" A small smile spreads across his lips as his eyes glow a bit brighter.

"Yes, but I was thinking more about Anthony."

Evander's eyes flash to Onyx's rapidly dimming eyes. "Anthony? Who was that?"

Onyx can hardly hide the snarl that forms on his face as he rolls his eyes in almost an otherworldly-fashion. "A humanoid who helped her. That's all. Nothing more to report than that."

"Is that true, Luna?"

Luna smiles and shrugs. "I really felt safe, when he was taking care of me before you got there. I will be forever grateful for that."

"You know, he'll be dead before you know it."

"What?" Luna's eyes grow wide as Evander face-palms audibly next to her.

"Well, you know human lives are fragile, and don't last for very long. They're not immortal like us."

"Sure, I suppose, but, I didn't want to think about his untimely death…"

"Well, it's going to happen, you know. Just you wait. Then who's going to take care of you, huh?"

The words from Onyx's mouth seethe from his cracking lips. Luna recoils from the kickback as Evander pats her awkwardly on the back. "Luna, why don't you head home and get some sleep? You've been here for quite a while, you're probably exhausted."

Luna nods, as fresh tears form at the corners of her eyes. "Uh, okay. I will. See you later, Onyx."

"Goodbye, *my love*." The words oozed from his lips like venom, clearly emphasized deliberately to make a point. Luna turns and walks slowly out of the Grand Hall. Onyx and Evander sit in utter silence until Luna's petite form makes its complete journey to the main door of the Grand Hall, and then takes a left turn to get onto the main pathway toward the habitation pods.

CHAPTER 8

"I have faith that you will adapt to your circumstances, somehow..." Rafaela wipes away one of my stray tears, even though I promised myself I wouldn't cry.

"I have no idea how though. I'm trapped, and there's no way out. My whole future... just gone. I don't want him and I don't see how I'll manage to be happy with him at all. It disgusts me. I don't want his children, I don't think I really want any at all, at least not yet. I'm scared, Rafaela."

She had become an older sister of sorts for me, almost a more free-living version of myself, even. Rafaela always has such an interesting style, both in what she wears and the way she lives. Letting myself melt into her arms was soothing in ways that I couldn't explain. I don't get that kind of love at home. My parents are good people and I know they care about us deeply, but I wouldn't consider myself to have a close relationship with them, really at all. Surely if I did, they wouldn't be forcing me into a union that would undoubtedly make me incredibly unhappy.

"Chin up, Constance. Things will get better. I look at it this way: you can either mourn the life you thought you wanted, and make yourself absolutely miserable, or you can embrace what has been offered you, and try to find joy in that. It's hard, believe me, I know." She pauses to toss her beautiful, shiny, midnight hair over her shoulder. "You can find joy in this. It will come. Just open your heart and your mind up to the possibilities." She pulls me close once more. "Don't get me wrong, this does break my heart on your behalf. I hate seeing you like this. But you'll find a way. You always do." She smiles at me, and I catch a glimpse of her sparkling eyes through the haze of my own tear-covered ones.

"Thank you, Rafaela. It's just… a lot to process. I can't believe I have to submit myself to that…" I look around to make sure we're alone. "… that lumpy, fat, and annoying man. I thought, I thought maybe I deserved better."

She sighs at my outburst, but the twinkle remains in her eyes. "You know what, Constance? I think you probably do. I think you absolutely deserve better. You can believe that. And every day, living with your betrothed, you can remind yourself that you are a princess living in unfortunate circumstances. And maybe, he'll turn into a prince, over time. It's far from ideal, sweetie. And I don't want to seem callous or unfeeling. I promise I'm none of those things. You know that, right?"

I manage to nod and smile politely, even though I feel like reality is crashing down on me with a thousand tons of misery.

"So you understand, I'm only trying to encourage you to make the best of what you have. There's really no other option, that is, unless you decide to run away…"

I look down at the ground, moving a pebble around with the toe of my shoe. "You think I could pull that off?"

Rafaela moves back to her display and pauses. "I was only joking, Constance. I wouldn't seriously suggest running away, absolutely not."

"Why though? You manage well enough on your own. Why couldn't I?"

She sighs, looking off sadly into the distance. "It's a long, painful story, Constance. Not sure I can bear to tell it right now."

"Oh, okay." But I'd be lying if I didn't admit my interest was quite piqued at this particular moment.

"Well what if I just travel around with you? Would you mind? Can we just go far away from here so they can't force me to marry that miserable lug?"

She smiled sweetly at me, and I notice the way her many bangle bracelets jingle in the warm early-morning breeze. "As much as I would like that, I couldn't live with myself if I took you away from your family without their consent - you're still under their domain, unfortunately."

I shrugged. "I suppose you're right. But I still would do just about anything if there was a way out of this."

She rubs my shoulder in sympathy. "Well, how long do you have until the wedding?"

I blow some hair out of my eyes. "I'm *betrothed* to be married in about two week's time."

"Well, here's what I'd do if I were you. You have fourteen days before you are bound to someone else forever. If there is something you've been wanting to do that you wouldn't be able to do then..." She pauses to wink at me, and I'm all too familiar with what she's hinting at. "I'd say now is the time for that. Do everything you can to make *now* worthwhile, so that you'll at least have some special memories to get you through your future."

I smirk a little, not even bothering to sensor my own mind as Mother had taught me. I figure it no longer matters, and it might just be a small act of defiance that the other things are coming to mind. "Thank you, Rafaela. I'm feeling... slightly more at peace with this. I'm still upset, and I still doubt that I'll ever be all that happy about it, but it's looking more feasible than it was. And for that, I thank you greatly."

She hugs me again. "I am so happy to hear that. I'd better get back to running my stand, but do come back next week to say hello. I need to give you a wedding present as well."

"Oh, you really don't have to -"

"Nonsense! It's still a celebration. I'm determined to make this special for you, even though it's not ideal. You'll see." She winks at me, and I find myself smiling back, legitimately this time.

"Well, that's quite kind of you. Oh, I'd better be getting back too." I look up at the sky, and the deep purple has turned to medium blue at this point, which means I'll be due back at my house in a matter of minutes before anyone starts wondering where I went.

"See you later, Rafaela!"

"May you be blessed, Constance."

I run a lot faster through the marketplace, and I completely forget to watch where I'm going until I run straight into someone's ample belly.

"Hey, watch where you're going!" I look up, and recognize the voice I'm going to be getting to know a *lot* better.

"Oh, my apologies, Silas." I bow my head, and look away.

"That's no problem, *my love*." The words hit me in the face and begin mocking me themselves. He reaches out to place his sweaty hand on my shoulder and I shake it off. His breath reeks of onions and garlic bread.

"I'm not *anything* to you for another two weeks. So don't call me anything." I stomp away, fighting the urge to kick him where I know it would hurt. I overhear him mumble the word "feisty" as I leave, and I smile to myself.

Oh he has no idea how 'feisty' I can be... but something tells me he's going to find out.

CHAPTER 9

"Griffin, go find Constance again. We need eyes on her at all times, so that you don't miss the defining moment coordinates."

"Roger that. I believe her house is just across the field I slept in, so she shouldn't be far. I just have to avoid being spotted this time."

"Exactly. Good luck, Griffin."

He clicks off his communicator, and then begins walking across the field as nonchalantly as possible, which is quite difficult in a very prominent light blue full-body jumpsuit amidst a Puritan compound. After a few minutes of dodging stares as much as he can, Griffin makes it to the back of Constance's house, and finds a good vantage point at the back window. Balancing on a stray wooden barrel, he manages to reach the bottom of the slightly ajar window. Inside the house, he sees a family going about their morning routine, until the front door opens and Constance hurriedly walks in.

"Constance! Where were you? And *where* is your head covering?"

Her mother seems quite upset at her for some reason. Oh no - has the moment already happened? Did I miss it in my lack of foresight?

"Sorry, Ma. I just went for a walk, to clear my head. And I... forgot it."

Her mother appears to click her tongue in protest, but she doesn't press the matter any more.

"All right, we can talk about this later. Go wash up for breakfast, now."

Griffin releases a breath he didn't realize he was holding, and then sits down on the barrel, facing the field he slept in overnight. He doesn't want to be caught by the family, so he decides not to risk looking through the window too long.

"Hey Nobody!"

Griffin groans with frustration as he looks to his left, and meets the mischievous gaze of the small child who had tormented him yesterday.

"Get away from me. You have no business here."

The child rolls his eyes. "Well, actually, I do. Ma sent me over here to ask Goody Miller for some butter. Then I saw you hiding out over here, so I came on back."

"Well, go do that then. I have no idea what you want with me, but I am here for very important work. Goodbye!"

Griffin decides to chance another look into the window again, and much to his disdain, the child climbs on his back.

"Get off of me." Griffin whispers as to not arouse suspicion from inside the house.

"But I gotta see what you're looking at. Oh... do you have a crush on Constance?"

"What? What is a *crush*?" Griffin takes the opportunity to shake the child off of his back, who falls to the dewy grass with a small thud, but remains unfazed.

"It means, you wanna kiss her or something." The nauseating child waggles his fingers in Griffin's general direction, as if to cast some sort of a spell on him.

"I am fairly certain that is not the case. Move along, now." He reaches for the window again, but the child latches onto his leg again. "Oh, not this again! You are utterly despicable and odd. It's a pity your mother puts up with you."

"Oh, Ma! She's probably looking for her butter! Well, I should go get that for her. See ya later, Nobody."

Griffin audibly exhales as the treacherous child lets go of his leg and disappears around the side of the simple, small home. Leaving him alone to his very important task, Griffin again manages to peek in the window without the family detecting him. But his efforts are mostly in vain, as the family appears to be eating breakfast in almost complete silence. The only sounds he can hear are coming from the infant humanoid at the end of the table as his mother silently feeds him some sort of lumpy-looking food.

"Well, is no one going to speak this morning? I was not made aware of any vows of silence in effect." The father in the house made an interesting comment, but no one besides his wife seemed to hear him. *How odd that is. Have the children spontaneously gone deaf?*

"It seems, there is just a lot going on in their minds right now, Ezekial. We'd best let them be." She motions to her two daughters, the elder of which seems especially withdrawn, while her younger sister seems to be quiet more in solidarity than with a concern of her own.

"Perhaps. But I would also appreciate the chance to socialize with my children before a long day in the fields."

Griffin notices Constance continuing to sit in utter silence, despite her father clearly wanting to speak to her.

"Ezekial, it seems they have fallen silent at the moment. Pray leave them be, I am certain this too shall pass."

The patriarch of the family grumbles a bit before angrily tossing his napkin on the table and storming out through the front door.

Griffin turns away from the window momentarily, once again feeling like an unwanted interloper for spying, especially on something so personal and private. Clicking on his communication device, he decides to ask Evander about it again.

"Evander, remind me again what exactly I'm looking for? I'm just watching her eat breakfast in silence at the moment, and I don't totally see the point of that."

"Griffin, any moment at all, could be *the moment* when history changed. You've got to be as vigilant as you can and watch for that. Tell me the time coordinates as soon as you see them on your external device, okay? This is of extreme importance."

He sighs. "Evander, I know. Believe me, I do. I just feel rather out of place doing this."

"Well of course you're out of place! You're an immortal Upperworld being spying on a teenage female humanoid in Puritan America. Of *course* you're out of place. But that's no reason to avoid your task. Both Onyx and Luna are relying on you. The Upperworld is no longer in jeopardy as it was, but there's still a major problem at hand. And there's something I haven't told you that has been a development since you've been gone."

"Oh?"

"Onyx is... becoming irritable, and the side effects of the throne are coming to the forefront. He is in a lot of discomfort, and his body isn't handling the current as well as we'd like. I haven't told Luna anything about this as I don't want to scare her, but I'm worried it might overtake him."

"Wow. That's... concerning."

"Indeed. So we need to get those coordinates, and then get you back here as soon as we can. Got it?"

"Yes, of course. I'll just try to become more comfortable with being uncomfortable, I guess."

"That's all you can do. And I think I speak on behalf of Luna and Onyx when I say they are extremely grateful to you for this."

"It is my honor to serve. I'll talk to you later, I should keep moving before that pesky humanoid finds me a third time."

"There was a *second* time?"

"Well, yes, but it was nothing to concern yourself with. Just keep on being there for Luna and Onyx. They need you too, I'm sure."

Evander sighs. "Will do. Over and out."

CHAPTER 10

"You shouldn't have said that to her, you know."

"Oh really? And why not?"

Evander sighs. "You can't see that she's distraught enough not being able to touch you and seeing you in so much discomfort? Why would you make her feel worse?"

"Because I feel worse than she does. I don't recall noticing her hair burning her scalp or her glowing eyes giving her migraines. And she's still mobile... she can walk around and do whatever she wants. I am stuck here, Evander. This was never what I wanted."

"I know that, Onyx. That's why we are working tirelessly to set you free, don't you know that? That's why Griffin is *risking* his own life by time-traveling, and we don't even have any real idea what could happen from that because it's never even been done before. You don't see that? You know, for a retracted humanoid who has the capacity to read emotions better than just about anyone else in the Upperworld, you'd think you'd understand. But no - you are just as callous and bitter as Zephyr himself was."

"Don't you *dare* say that to me!" Onyx's eyes and hair both grow as bright as Evander has ever seen them. Onyx winces under the extra heat and burning he feels.

"I will say whatever I want to you! We're supposed to be close friends, Onyx. We've worked alongside each other for centuries! So, I will tell you whatever I want and as uncomfortable as it is, I will say what needs to be said.

Well, anything short of unseemly Earth jargon, because you know how I feel about that."

Onyx's gaze softens as he realizes how harsh he must sound, but the pain and worry he feels quickly upsets him again.

"That may be so, but regardless, I have never been so distraught in all my centuries of existence."

"Oh, you don't know the half of it." Evander sighs. "Onyx, have you seen a mirror recently?"

"What do you mean?"

Evander motions for a nearby screen to detach from the wall it is usually stored on, and then moves it closer to the throne. With a click of a button, Evander turns it on and sets it on Reflect Mode, so that it can show Onyx what he looks like.

"Evander... what's happening to me?" His voice softens completely now, at a loss for what he's seeing. It's undeniable now, what's happening to him. His skin is almost completely pale now, and his glowing eyes have started to sink a little deeper into his head, with dark shadows all around them.

"Onyx, the current is overtaking you. We didn't know this would happen, and we were hoping it wouldn't. But I'm thinking it's because you weren't predestined to hold this position."

"Is it... permanent?"

"As long as you are on that throne, I'd say so."

His hair and eyes dim significantly as a single tear slides down his cheek. "Does Luna know?"

"I've refrained from telling her anything, it's not worth it to upset her at this point."

"But she has a right to know!"

Evander rubs the back of his neck as he pauses. "Be that as it may, I worry that information of that nature would put her into a very unhealthy emotional state. She's still doing very important work in the Sorting Room, you know. And the last thing we need is another malfunction."

Onyx opens his cavernous mouth to speak, but no sound comes out. Instead, he just closes it, nods almost imperceptibly, and then slumps back in his chair.

"I am grateful to you, Evander."

"For what?"

"For taking care of her when I can't."

"It is my honor, my friend. And while we're on the subject of that, I hate to say it but perhaps your outburst toward her earlier was a little uncalled for?"

His hair glows a bit brighter, and his eyes widen in embarrassment. "Well, no! I mean, she was with that Earthling for a while. And he was, helping her, I guess. But I should have been the one to be there with her! I hate that he... got that time with her that I didn't."

Evander shrugs. "I suppose, but like you said - he's going to die, and you're not, so who has the upper hand, really?"

Onyx frowns at the harshness of his own words. "Well, when you put it that way, it's a bit morbid, don't you think?"

"Well, you're the one who mentioned it first."

"I know, I'm kidding, Evander."

"Kidding?"

"Yes, that's humanoid speak for... oh never mind."

"Okay, fair enough."

The two friends just stare at each other in silence for a few moments, wondering what they should do or say next.

"You know, it's going to be okay. I don't want you to worry, Onyx. We'll find a way, somehow."

"I appreciate you saying that, Evander. But I really doubt that you can, at this point."

"What do you mean? We have Griffin watching your mother for any signs of choosing to alter the narrative, and those coordinates are going to set you free -"

"Maybe. You mean *maybe* they'll set me free. It's all theoretical, isn't it? You really have no idea if it's actually going to work. For all I know, I might really be stuck here indefinitely. Right? Tell me if I'm wrong, but I don't think I am."

Evander looks down at his feet, suddenly finding the spotless white marble floor of the Grand Hall to be much more interesting than conversation. "I guess... you're not wrong."

"Exactly. So stop pretending it's definitely going to work, because we just don't know that yet and I don't want to get my hopes up. Most importantly, I don't want Luna to get her hopes up just to be disappointed."

Evander slowly nods, and then turns to walk out of the Grand Hall.

CHAPTER 11

"Girls, you shall not ignore your father like that. What has gotten into you both?"

I exchange a tired, sad glance at my sister, who has the same sort of blank stare on her face. Baby Jedidiah just keeps eating his mush breakfast, always the oblivious one. I take it upon myself to speak, even though I really don't want to.

"We're both... processing what was discussed yesterday."

Mother nods, and uncomfortably looks out the window. "I see. Well, do be more respectful to your father in the future." She doesn't press the matter, and I can tell that she likely isn't thrilled for me either. Unfortunately, fathers often chose husbands for their daughters. Mothers don't seem to have any real say in it once a deal has been made and hands have shook. I know that all too well now.

"Well, what are you girls planning for today? Have you done your chores yet?"

I nod, even though I haven't. I'm in no mindset for chores and I don't plan on forcing myself to do anything I don't want to, at least for the next two weeks. They'll own me after that, but for now, I am my own. Probably for the last time ever.

"Yes Mother, I already collected the eggs from the chickens, milked the cow, and swept the barn floor."

Mother smiles at Fae. "Thank you very much, Fae." Then she picks up Jedidiah and disappears out of the kitchen and into her bedroom, likely to freshen up for the day.

"So what are you doing today, Constance?"

I smirk at her. "Absolutely anything and everything I want."

Fae's eyes widen. "What exactly do you mean?"

I wink at her. "They may own me in two weeks, but for now, I am all mine. And I intend to make the most of the time I have."

She tilts her head. "And is Ma and Pa okay with that?"

I fight the urge to laugh in her face. "That's just the ticket, Fae - they don't get a say in the matter. I don't get a say in the matter of my marriage to that miserable lump of goo and fat, so they don't get a say about what I do for the next two weeks. And I have found a great deal of peace in that sentiment. For the next two weeks, I am *taking* my life back, Fae. And I've never been happier."

Fae's eyebrows seem to make a run to hide in her overgrown bangs. "Well, uh, okay Constance. Whatever you need to do, I guess that makes sense." She gets up from the table and goes toward our bedroom, and then returns momentarily with my head covering. "Oh, and you forgot this earlier this morning. Here you go." She hands it to me, and I promptly let it fall onto the kitchen table. You'd think it was laced with poison, the way that garment makes me feel. But I opt to wear it anyway in broad daylight, as I'm going out today and don't necessarily want any extra attention on me.

Then I walk right out the front door of our house, and put my sights on Finn's house. I think it's time I just told him how I feel. It's now or never, quite literally. I smile and wave politely at our neighbors, even the nauseating Johnson family as all their obnoxious children seem to be loudly fighting in the back of their wagon on the way to market.

And then, I reach the door right near my own home, and look around the yard for his familiar head of medium-brown hair crowning a gorgeous face and a muscular body. I'd recognize him anywhere. He's the kind of person that I barely allowed myself to admire for a long time, as mother told me those urges were wrong at my age and that I should go spend more time at church instead. But now, you'd better believe I didn't care about any of that anymore. I'd still have to be strategic about it though.

I spot him hoeing the soil for planting, likely trying to get the brunt of the physical labor done before the sun gets to the height of its heat for the day. His eyes meet mine, squinting a bit to keep the rising sun out of them. I manage to smile and wave, blushing and relaxing my posture a little as the warm breeze gently tugs at my skirt.

He immediately pauses his work and walks over to me. I notice for the millionth time the way every one of his muscles flexes and relaxes in sync - the boy himself is a beautiful, mechanized wonder. I feel my face heating up, and I quickly look away, hoping the blood collecting under the skin of my rosy cheeks dissipates soon.

"Good morning, Constance."

I look back at him, and meet his gaze, swallowing the lump in my throat and hoping he can't hear how fast my heart is beating.

"Good morning, Finn." We stare at each other wordlessly for a minute, Finn wiping some sweat off of his already-moist forehead, and me breaking eye contact while suddenly finding my shoes to be the most interesting matter at the moment.

"Did you come by for something? Need some sugar again like last week?"

I smile but shake my head. "No, it's not that."

"No? Well then did your pa need to borrow another tool of some sort?"

"No, it's not that either."

He shrugs his shoulders. "Well, what is it, then?" He scratches the back of his head, awaiting my answer. But even I didn't know how to give it to him. So I say something borderline ridiculous, because I ran out of things to stall with."

"Come with me."

I can see a smile pulling at the edges of his lips. "Come with you where? I was just doing some yard work…" He's hesitating to agree to just drop everything, but I think I know how to get him away from it for a a little while, at least.

"Just come with me, please? I just… wanted to show you my favorite thinking spot."

"A thinking spot, you say? And what exactly would we be… thinking about?" He takes another step closer to me, letting his breath mingle with my own more frequent exhales.

"Anything. Anything at all. It's just nice to... get away from all the chores, and expectations sometimes, wouldn't you agree?"

He shrugs his shoulders. "I wouldn't know, I guess I've never really been away from it." He pauses to look back at his house, and nods.

"You'll come with me?"

"Sure. I guess I could use a break. I've been working like a dog the past few days."

I smile, and start walking down the road wordlessly. I hear his hurried footfalls follow mine, and try not to blush when I feel the warmth of his hand find my own.

CHAPTER 12

Griffin watches as Constance walks off away from her house, with a boy in tow. Not completely sure what to make of that, he opts to follow them - while remaining incognito, of course. And staying under the radar has become even more difficult as of late, since the young humanoid has been pestering him. Regardless of the past annoyance the young humanoid has caused, Griffin resigned himself to follow Constance by casually walking along the buildings and trying to blend in with the growing foot traffic and midmorning noise. Just as his shoulders relax a bit and he starts to actually breathe again without panicking too much about being noticed, the unthinkable happens.

"You! You're the one my son has been talking about!"

Griffin turns around to see a very harried mother staring him down with her hands on her hips, flanked by a stained and wrinkled apron. her hair is bedraggled as well, with curls springing all around her face like an angry lioness. "I am not so sure what you mean. I must be going now, though." He tries to turn away, but no such luck - the woman has her hand clamped tightly around his wrist. *What is it with this family and their death grips?*

"You're coming with me."

"Unhand me now, peasant!"

Her eyes widen at the insinuation he makes, but her mouth doesn't utter a sound. But at that moment, Griffin becomes as confident as he ever has.

"Let me go. You have no business torturing me. I have done *nothing* to warrant such an interrogation." He intensifies his gaze, suddenly emboldened by his time on Earth - or perhaps his desperation has strengthened him.

She begrudgingly lets go, tossing his arm to his side with palpable frustration. "Stay away from my children. Stay away from my family. And most importantly…" She steps uncomfortably close to Griffin, and he winces at the rotten smell of her breath. "Stay away from me." Turning on her heel, Griffin is once again alone. But he has a sinking feeling that he most likely won't be for long. Unfortunately, however, this encounter had held him up long enough to allow Constance to move farther down the path and out of his sight.

Just wonderful. Now I have no idea where she is or where she's going. Now what do I do?

Griffin looks around in frustration, simultaneously upset that he lost his target, but also that he's still stuck in the open, where he could be discovered yet again. Finding a nearby structure, he decides to hide in there until he can figure out what to do next.

They can't be too far away, I bet I can find them. I just have to keep looking. Yes, that's it - I'll just keep looking.

He tries to ready himself with some deep breaths, but the stress of his mission and the expectations that

132

surround it are starting to get to him. Sitting down against the wooden wall of the structure, he rests his head in his hands and hopes that he'll figure out what to do before it's too late. Letting down Onyx and Luna is not an option he wants to consider. Unfortunately, reality rarely, if ever, follows his preferences. And Griffin is just about to find out how very true that is.

***

"Evander? Are you all right?" He turns around to meet Brielle's kind gaze. The younger sorter smiles at him, but concern remains in her eyes. "I'm no expert on emotion, and I know you don't have a capacity for it any more than I do, but you look upset. Just a guess". She shrugs her shoulders as if to punctuate her point, and her calm exhales mingle with the purple fog of the Upperworld.

"Oh, Brielle... yes, I'll be just fine. I mean, I am fine. Trust me, I'm not the one worthy of worry."

She tilts her head to the side, and gently tugs Evander by his sleeve toward a nearby tree, out of the main traffic and earshot of the busy pathway. "What do you mean, exactly? Someone is in trouble?"

Evander opens his mouth to speak, and then shuts it. His hand rubs the back of his neck nervously. Trying to figure out how much should be revealed, and who it should be revealed to, often left him more perplexed than the actual problem at hand. He always theorizes that it's just a part of being a record-keeper, as if his own thoughts and experiences were locked away in their own drawer inside his head.

"Evander? Earth to Evander! What's wrong with you? You're completely out of it." She snaps her fingers in front of his face, and his immediate surroundings come back into focus.

"I'm really sorry, Brielle. There's been a lot going on, and there's just so much to consider."

She nods, and then recognition floods her face. "Oh my pod, is it Griffin? Is he in danger?"

"No, not at the moment. He seems to be doing just fine, for the most part. You can come to the Grand Hall and keep an eye on him via the live feed, if you want."

She smiles but shakes her head. "Thanks, but I don't think I should. Sometimes watching those live feeds scare me more than they help me - you know, after seeing what happened with Luna…"

Evander nods, understanding Brielle's worry, since Luna had been through so much and much of it was such a clear example of the worst Earth had to offer her.

"So what were you so concerned about?"

Evander looks around her, avoiding eye contact with every fiber of his being. "Brielle, I really don't want to worry you. I can assure you, we are on top of things. Don't burden yourself with it, really."

She nods, but remains standing resolutely in front of him. Her hesitation to move and continue going about her day was the last straw for Evander's resolve. Against his own better judgement, he allowed her to break him.

"If you really must know, I suppose I can tell you. But not here. Come with me back to my record keeping office, and we can talk there."

Brielle's small smile creeped across her face, and she nods enthusiastically. "Thank you, Evander."

"You're welcome, as long as that's truly what you want."

"It is. I feel... so completely wrapped up in these happenings, even though I haven't been completely involved in them, I feel connected somehow. You are all, my friends."

"I should have thought so. I apologize for hesitating. But you're about to see why I did."

CHAPTER 13

"You still haven't told me where we're going." Finn's voice, as soft as velvet but as strong as a springtime mare hits my ears amidst the warm spring breeze. I smile back at him, trailing slightly behind me as I pick up my pace.

"We're almost there, just keep moving." I hear his throaty laughter and feel my laugh explode out of my throat. Something about him, and the way he responds to life and the unknown, has always enchanted me in the best way. Maybe that's part of the reason I never could get him out of my head. And it was just recently when I finally decided to stop trying.

His clammy palm gently squeezes mine, and I lead him to my favorite spot in the whole world. Or, at least the world as we know it.

"Okay, this is it."

I pause to take in the scenery - that is, the view, and the boy looking at it with me. The two of us are standing under a tree at the top of the hill, overlooking the entire compound.

"Wow, this is... pretty amazing. We're so far away from everything, but also, so close at the same time. And the sky... it feels so wide open."

I smile, and then nod. "That's pretty much why I love this spot. Sometimes I bring a good book and some lunch to eat while I spend a few hours reading. It's heavenly, really."

He smiles at me, and then shrugs. "How in the world do you manage to get time for that? Pa always keeps me busy, whether it's helping in the yard, or watching my sister if Ma needs me to. There's usually no time for anything."

I smirk at him, and then lean a little closer as if to tell him a secret, even though we're completely alone and no one could hear me anyway. "That's just the ticket - I don't tell them. because then, that'd give them a chance to give me some mundane task to do."

He laughs out loud, bending back in a full-blown stroke of hilarity. "I will never understand where you get your bravery, Constance. It's so... genius. But you're also asking for it, you know."

"What?" I tilt my head to the side, and wait for his explanation.

"Yeah, I mean, you don't wait for permission to be given. You just... take it."

I pause for a minute, deciding how much I should tell him. "Well, it's more fun that way."

"That is certainly true, I suppose." I watch as his face crinkles into a broad grin, and then he looks back out to the compound beneath and stretching out in front of us.

An uncomfortable silence descends on us out of the blue, and I shuffle my feet nervously trying to figure out what to do next.

"You know, the view is better from the tree."

"You climb that tree?"

Now I'm the one laughing incredulously. "No, no, I just sit under it. Come here, I'll show you."

I don't even hesitate to grab his hand and lead him toward the very inner sanctum of my favorite spot. I pat down a section of grass next to me and pull him down onto it. He nearly loses his balance in the process though, and almost lands on top of me.

"Oh my, sorry, Constance. I didn't mean to…"

"You don't have to apologize to me, Finn. I brought you here, so it's my fault if the grass was slippery or something."

"It wasn't slippery, I just…" He shrugs, suddenly realizing how useless that topic has become. "Nevermind, it's just nice to be here with you, Constance. To see everything from a… new perspective."

"It is nice, isn't it?"

He nods, and the silence creeps up on us again, until I decide to break it as unceremoniously as possible.

"Don't you wish we could just escape it all?"

"Escape what?" He turns to face me, and I try not to get lost in his deep, shining eyes.

"This whole lifestyle. It's ridiculous, how we work, and work, and have families, until we die. Don't you want more from life than that?"

He sighs, looking out onto the compound again in the late morning air. "I suppose? I've never given much thought to it. But I see what you mean - it's quite dull, when you put it that way."

138

"Isn't it though! Believe me, I know. I'm already a commodity in the system, apparently."

"Whatever do you mean, Constance?"

I bite my lip in what I hope seems seductive, but I'm actually just nervous about how he might react to what I am about to admit. "There's been... an arrangement made for me."

"Really?"

I try to read the look on his face, expecting shock and repulsion, but instead, I sense something more akin to... disappointment. Was I imagining that part? I must have been. I had to have been.

"Yes, it's true."

He runs his hand through his hair. "Who is it?"

I sigh. Of course he's asking that. Maybe he's curious... or dare I say, maybe a little jealous? "It's Silas Brewster."

He shakes his head. "That's... something all right." He throws a small pebble down the hill, and we both watch it slowly pick up speed as it goes.

"It's unfortunate, is what it is."

"How so? Aren't you happy to have been given a match?"

The sarcasm in his voice is undeniable, but I think he is doing his best to be polite, at least on the surface. "No. I'm really not. Devastated, actually."

He turns to face me, and I swear his eyes are starting to sparkle again. "Really?"

"Completely. Silas is little more than a fat pig. I've met fruit flies with better personalities than his."

Finn laughs out loud, no longer trying to hide his reaction anymore. His smile fades as soon as it appears though. "I'm so sorry to hear about your situation, Constance. It's... upsetting, for sure. Have you talked to your ma and pa about how you're feeling about it?"

"Of course! But as you can only imagine, once I've been traded for livestock, there's no going back." I pause to lower my voice a bit more, as if to remind him how serious this is. "They *own* me, Finn. And there's nothing I can do about it. Don't you see? You get to have some say in who you end up with. I don't, and I never will. I'll be Silas' personal child producer in just under a couple of weeks."

He remains silent, looking off into the distance. "Is that why you brought me here? To tell me this?"

I swallow. He's probably embarrassed and uncomfortable. Or at least, very upset. "No... I mean, yes? No, I mean, not entirely. It just kind of happened."

"So you just accidentally told me that you're taken? Is that what you wanted me to know?"

I shake my head. "But you don't understand... I'm not taken, not yet, anyway."

"But you just said..."

"No, I said I *will be*. Not yet."

"Oh. Okay." He throws another pebble down the hill, angrier this time. "So why am I here, again?"

I don't bother answering him with words this time. Instead, I do something I've been wanting to do for years. I lean closer to him until a few strands of loose hair fall out of my bonnet. And then I kiss him.

Griffin continues walking down the pathway in the direction he saw them going before he was intercepted by the maternal humanoid earlier. *These people are so intense… it's not like I hurt the child, even if it was getting to the point where I was starting to want to, at least a little. But I wouldn't, of course. I couldn't. It would change the narrative, after all.*

After what feels like forever, Griffin finally sees a boy sitting under a tree with Constance next to him. He quickly finds a spot to hide where he can observe them without being noticed and changing anything.

"Onyx, I've got eyes on her again. It was a bit tricky after my path was diverted momentarily, but I managed to find them again." He waits for the connection to get through, as at the moment, he is met with nothing but some crackling static noise. "Onyx? Come in, Onyx? Onyx!" His breathing intensifies, but then he hears the static subside and Onyx picks up the communicator call.

"Griffin, sorry to worry you. I will have Evander look into strengthening the connection as soon as possible. I'm not sure why that happened."

"Oh, okay. But anyway, she's right here. And… oh. Oh my… I don't want to get you too high on hope but is this… the moment? She's… doing something… that I can't explain."

Onyx breathes in sharply, which transmits over the communicator. "Let me pull up the live feed." The screen swings out in the Grand Hall, and Onyx awaits to see more than he wants to of his mother. But then, he laughs to himself, as he sees that is clearly not the case. A sigh of relief escapes his lips.

"No Griffin, that's not the moment we need. No need to bother collecting the time coordinates. That's not it."

"Oh, it's not? Hmmm." He scratches his chin. "Well, perhaps you should describe to me, in detail, what it is exactly that I'm looking for?"

Onyx sighs audibly. "I told you, you need to find the moment that marks the time that -"

"- the time that the narrative was permanently changed. I know. What I don't know, exactly, is what that would *look* like."

Onyx's breath catches in his throat again. "Oh... that. Well, that's not something I feel at liberty to speak about." He lowers his voice, and a very bright blushing appears on his cheeks, even though Griffin can't see him and his face has become very pale since his time on the throne began.

"And why not? You want me to get the coordinates, right?"

"Yes, of course, but..."

"But what?" Griffin places a hand on his hip, even though Onyx can't see him and his frustrated posture.

"It's... something you wouldn't understand."

"Oh really? Try me."

✳✳✳

"Okay, no one can hear us in here. Can you tell me what's going on now?"

Evander checks the door lock and the soundproofing one last time, and then hesitantly settles himself in his well-worn desk chair. Motioning to Brielle to make herself comfortable, she drags a nearby chair in front of Evander and lays her hands daintily in her lap, awaiting the explanation she asked for.

"Well? I'm waiting."

"Okay, so here's what's going on. Onyx is being overtaken by the current."

"Is that bad?" She tosses some of her hair aside, and then resumes eye contact with Evander.

"Well it doesn't sound good, does it?"

She shakes her head. "What does that mean, exactly?"

"His body wasn't made for this kind of stress and strain. He's already started to break down. It looks to be only a matter of time until..."

"Until what?"

"Until... he meets a similar fate as Zephyr did."

"Oh, wow." She looks down at her feet, trying to swallow the news. "But Zephyr lasted for eons... Onyx hasn't been on the throne for very long."

"Perhaps. But Zephyr was a Titan, destined from the beginning of time to serve in the capacity that he did. Onyx... was not."

Brielle nods. "I suppose that's true. So... does that mean you'll need another replacement?"

Evander sighs. "I sure hope not. But if we can't get him off of that throne, we just may need one."

"Your plan is to set up a wireless connection for him, correct?"

"That *was* our plan, yes."

"That won't work now?"

Evander pauses, and rests his hand on his outstretched palm. "Well, yes, it could work. A wireless connection to the current would allow his body to exist and recover from the damage that was done, as he wouldn't need to be in direct contact with it anymore - rather, he would just wear a transmitter that would link it to his life-force."

"That sounds fine then."

"I suppose that does, yes. But there's no way to get him off of the throne until we get those time coordinates. And at the rate that he is degrading, we might not get those coordinates until it is too late."

"Oh." Brielle looks down at her feet nervously. "Does Luna know?"

"Not about him degrading as fast as he is. And she's not going to."

"Why not? I'm sure Onyx would want her to know."

"Actually Brielle, that's just the thing - he doesn't want her to know, because it would just worry her, and what good would that accomplish? If you have any care for Luna, and any respect for Onyx, you will listen to me, and you will respect his wishes. Understand?"

Brielle slowly nods, but she is clearly conflicted. "If I were Luna, I would definitely want to know."

"But you're not Luna, and you must remember that Luna and Onyx are part humanoid, and therefore have the capacity to experience emotion - we do not. Therefore, they don't process matters like this with logic - instead, they are often bogged down by their feelings. To maintain a sharp mind, and to keep her calm so that she can do her job, Onyx knows that she must not know. You *will* not tell her."

"Okay Evander. I promise."

He nods in agreement. "Good."

CHAPTER 15

Time slows down to a full stop. It's only a few seconds at best, maybe. But his lips on mine are everything I was hoping they'd be. He hesitated at first, but then seemed to reciprocate. I force myself to pull away so I can gauge how he's feeling. I'm met with his bright eyes shining brighter than I've ever seen them before.

"Constance... I. That was... why did... am I supposed to be..."

He continues to ramble on in short sentences for a few more moments, and I just can't stop smiling. "It's just something I wanted... for a really long time. I hope you didn't mind..."

He blushes quite visibly even though I know he's trying to hide it. "No. I definitely didn't mind."

"Really?"

"Yeah. I've actually... always thought quite highly of you, Constance."

"And I you, Finn."

We look at each other in silence, and I really want to kiss him again, but I refrain from that, as I don't want to overwhelm him or make things needlessly awkward, even if he did take it well the first time. I notice the rising temperatures, and decide to let my hair free of its cloth prison.

"Your hair... it's beautiful, Constance. I've never seen it..."

"Without the covering? I know. It's much too hot for it today anyway."

"Aren't you supposed to wear it though?"

I sigh, and flip my long blonde hair over my shoulder and smile as the breeze moves through it. "I'm supposed to do a lot of things, Finn. But that doesn't mean I plan on doing them."

He smirks at me, and I can't help but notice the way his face crinkles up and how very sweet he looks with that smile on his face.

"I don't know how you manage it."

"Manage what?"

He pauses to look out at the scenery before us, and the way the sun is rapidly making its ascent in the late morning sky. "You're such a good daughter. You do everything you're supposed to, mostly. And you're a teacher at the schoolhouse. They don't let just any girl do that - you have really good social standing in the compound. And then, you pull off stuff like this, and no one ever suspects a thing. You've never done anything really bad in your whole life, and yet you get away with almost anything you want. You are a complete mystery, Constance."

"I suppose. It's not like I plan these things out though. They just kind of happen."

He nods. "Well, I guess you finally met your match, anyway."

"I did?"

148

He nods, but I see a frown tugging at the edges of his mouth. "Your pa. You said he set you up with Silas, and there's no getting out of it."

I sigh as the adrenaline from kissing Finn wears off, and I come back to reality. "Yes, it appears so."

"So what's your plan?"

"There's no plan."

"Constance, you *always* have a plan. I always notice how you think up new ways to do things. You're inventive, and so creative. Remember that time when the Holden's cow refused to be milked and you came up with the idea to distract her with some sugar cubes? No one else would have figured out how to deal with a stubborn cow. Maybe your ma and pa are just like that."

I lean back on my elbows in the soft spring grass. Tilting my head from side to side, I let his words wash over me as the warm breeze mingles with the light perspiration on the back of my neck. "So my ma and pa are stubborn cows?" I laugh out loud at the thought, and Finn does too, but then he shakes his head.

"No, well, not exactly. I just mean..." He leans closer to me now, to whisper some words which could change everything for me. "It's possible that they might bend to your will if you find a good enough distraction for them."

"Theoretically, perhaps. But it may be a bit hard to distract them from the fact that their daughter is being married off in less than two weeks. I have to finish up my teaching by this coming Friday, and then after that, all the arrangements must be made."

"Arrangements?"

I nod. "I'm not at all looking forward to any of it. I think they expect me to meet with Silas to discuss where we're going to live and everything."

"Oh. That doesn't sound very good at all."

"That's for sure."

I nod, and try not to flinch as Finn inches a bit closer to me. "Do you think we should be getting back now? Before anyone wonders where we are? My pa might even be furious by now."

I sigh. I definitely don't want this moment to end, but I've seen how upset Finn's pa can get sometimes, and it's not a pleasant sight. I reluctantly nod, and then accept the hand Finn offers to me to help me up from the grass we were sitting on. He hoists me up but doesn't let go, pulling me closer just for a moment.

"Before we go, I just... wanted to remember this for what it's worth." And then he initiates our second kiss with his hand on my lower back, allowing us both to linger just a bit longer than we did before. I feel my whole body warm up, even though it's a rather nice spring day. His soft lips are coaxing all the emotions out of my own mouth that I would never be able to explain with words anyway. He breaks off our embrace as reluctantly as I did before, and then grabs my hand to lead me back to the main path.

"Was it worth it?" I pause momentarily to gauge his expression. The blush reanimates behind his suntanned face under medium brown hair.

"Absolutely. I didn't know what I was missing, now I just wish I knew sooner."

I sigh and watch my feet hitting the path next to him, his solid, strong gait slowed down just slightly to better match my own. "Knew what sooner?"

"I wish I knew... how deeply my feelings ran for you. I hesitated for way too long. I waited for years to say something."

"Oh." If there was ever a time to really begin to hate my family and their traditional expectations for me, it is now.

CHAPTER 16

"Oh, wow. So that's really what I'm looking for? I'm not sure... I really want to see that, Onyx. Sounds... unpleasant and rather disgusting." Griffin looks down at the ground, and manages to follow Constance and Finn from a distance as they walk back home from the cliffside.

"Yes Griffin, it has to be *that*. It's not guaranteed that it will be the moment we need, but I'm going to need to at least try those coordinates in case they are the ones that work. If not those, then perhaps you'll try the ones a few days after."

Griffin sighs through the receiver. "What happens a few days after?"

"Well, according to what I am expecting, I believe that she's going to be made aware of the presence of the fetus. At which point, she'll decide to... terminate it."

"You mean you? You're the fetus, right?" Griffin waits for Onyx's response, and regrets saying what he did as he realizes that he may have crossed a line.

"Was. I *was* the fetus. But that's not important for your task, Griffin. Just keep an eye on her, and let me know what coordinates your communication device displays at those moments."

"Okay, I understand, Onyx. I will do my best."

Onyx clicks off without saying goodbye this time, which makes his distaste obvious to Griffin. He makes a mental note to himself to apologize to Onyx next time they speak.

The scenery is quite pleasant this time of day, and Griffin has to remind himself to stay focused on the task at hand. He has now mostly adapted to the differing gravity levels and environment, so he's able to operate on Earth in relative comfort at this point. He approaches the compound while following the duo he's been sent to monitor, and waits for the next notable thing to happen. As they get closer to the houses, he manages to duck in and out of sheds and other convenient hiding spots.

"Who are you?"

He turns around to find himself face-to-face with Constance herself, with Finn standing close behind her. "Huh? Oh, I'm no one. Just carry on." He quickly tries to run away, but the boy grabs his shoulder and prevents him from making a hasty getaway.

"I thought I could sense someone following us. I wasn't sure but now I am. Who are you?"

Griffin begins to panic, as he realizes how detrimental and potentially dangerous it is to come into direct contact with the very people he has been sent to observe. "I'm not following *you*." He emphasizes that slight detail, hoping that the loophole he found would be enough to get them off his tail without having to outright lie.

"Oh really? Then why did I feel eyes on us? Are you working for her pa?" Finn tightens his grip on Griffin's shoulder.

"What? Who's 'Pa'? And why would I be working for him? Please let go of me, I promise I don't have any ill will toward anyone. Please." Griffin tries to smile at him reassuringly, but to no avail.

"I'm not convinced. Constance, you said you saw this guy around recently, right? Are you sure it's the same guy?"

The girl nods nervously. "Of course! Who else do you know who dresses like that?" She motions to Griffin's Upperworld jumpsuit, instantly making him wish that he bothered to procure some more Earth-typical clothing before embarking on his quest.

"That's true, I've never even seen clothes like that before."

The girl looks Griffin up and down, analyzing his every move and nuance. Griffin winces at the thought of the way his image was being imprinted in her memory. He starts thinking up ways to get away, but nothing good comes to mind. He could try to shove the boy's hand off of his shoulder, but he'd have to sprint away which could call even more attention to him, and perhaps even start a fight. None of that would be good.

"Look, I have no idea why you're here or what you want, but I'm going to say this once and only once." The boy leans in menacingly toward Griffin. "Stay away from me and *my girl*. Got it?"

Griffin nods, and then backs away when his shoulder is finally released from the death grip supplied by the curious humanoid.

✷✷✷

Brielle exits Evander's record-keeping office feeling a new weight on her shoulders. It's always tough to know information that will undoubtedly be of concern to someone but be forbidden to reveal it to them. But that is what she promised Evander, and she would have to stick with that, no matter how badly she feels about it. Running to her own pad, she decides to spend some time alone to ponder what she's been forced to swallow.

Upon arriving, she opens her door and lets herself in, and then flops down on her very plush bed. *Luna would be upset, of course. But if I were her, I'd be a lot more upset not to know the truth. But I did promise Evander. I wish he didn't make me promise that.*

Her thoughts swirl inside her head, and without anything else to do, she resigns herself to taking a nap. But sleep runs from her faster than her torturous thoughts are whirling around in her mind.

What if I just tell Luna only what she needs to know? That Onyx has a limited amount of time? Maybe she'd be able to help somehow. I wouldn't want to limit our options, and she has a lot more experience with this stuff than I do. If she can help, she ought to know what's going on.

Satisfied with that rationale, she finally manages to go to sleep. But the coming concern surrounding telling Luna how the love of her life is rapidly failing fills her with dread, and she tosses and turns the whole time.

CHAPTER 17

"You... you called me *your* girl?" I looked at Finn standing next to me and can't keep the smile from spreading over my face. He shuffles his feet in the dust of the road and nods almost imperceptibly.

"I guess I did."

"But I'm -"

"- betrothed to Silas. I know."

I nod at him, and then excuse myself to enter my house alone so that my family wouldn't pester me with all kinds of nosy questions. He waves at me as I turn away, and I pray silently that the blush forming on my cheeks would dissipate before my parents question me about it. Then again, if they were planning on taking the rest of my life from me, then there was no reason why I couldn't at least own these last couple weeks for myself.

"Constance! Where have you been? We were looking for you earlier. Your chores still need to be done." My mother faces me with her hands placed staunchly on her hips, and I have to force myself to avoid rolling my eyes at her. No need to pick any extra fights besides the all-encompassing betrothal fight. That one would be quite enough for the ages.

"I just went for a walk in the fresh spring air, Ma. It's really beautiful out today."

She nods, but her distaste with me remains apparent. "I understand, but did you need to take all morning? Was that absolutely necessary?"

156

I shake my head no, but clench my fist inside the pocket of my dress.

"And where is your head covering? Did you walk around outside with your hair uncovered like that?"

I reach up to touch the top of my head, and freeze as I realize that I must have left my head covering on the cliffside. "Oh my, it seems I must have. Sorry, Ma. I'll go get another one from my room." I disappear into the room I share with Fae so that I can recover my hair before Ma feels the need to lecture me for the thousandth time about saving my tresses for my husband and all that traditional stuff that I've always hated so much.

"Constance! Keep that one on this time, please."

I nod my affirmation, and then grab the broom out of the closet to tidy up the floor as I usually do on Saturday mornings. Ma resumes kneading some dough in the kitchen, and Pa is likely working in the fields again. Fae must have already finished her chores, as she is sitting at the table doing some of her schoolwork.

"Constance, I need help with this arithmetic problem, can you help me?" I pause my tidying to help her with the problem, even though my own problems are still at the forefront of my mind.

"Sure, Fae! What seems to be troubling you?"

She begins to ask me some questions about the latest long division problem she is working on, and I help her the best I can. I almost forget about how angry I am at our parents until Ma says something I didn't know would rattle me as much as it did:

"Oh my, Constance, you are going to be such a handsome mother to Silas' children!"

She stands there smiling at me, clapping her hands slightly. That comment fills my blood with venom, and I simply decide to stand there in front of her, maintaining silent eye contact until she backs off.

"Well, perhaps it's a bit early to expect that of you. Nothing until your wedding night, of course, anyway!" She tries to balance my discomfort with some levity, but I remain as stone-faced as a statue. Fae pauses her arithmetic work to view the spectacle that is unfolding in front of her. Ma's smile rapidly fades, and she turns back to her kitchen work as I continue working with Fae.

After I finish helping Fae with her schoolwork, I resume my chores until I hear some commotion outside my window. In fact, it looks like a fight is breaking out. Before Ma or Fae can stop me, I run straight out our house to see what's going on.

"I saw *you* with Constance earlier today, don't even try to tell me you weren't!" Fat, smelly Silas is holding Finn by his shirt collar in the middle of the street.

"What do you mean? We just went for a walk, nothing happened!" Finn throws a couple of useless punches before just giving up and trying to reason with him. Silas' belly fat functions like armor, and very few people can punch hard enough to hurt him in his midsection.

"Oh please, Finn. No one goes for 'just a walk' with *that* girl. Now admit it so I can make you sorry!"

I can see Finn wincing from Silas' rank breath, and I feel instantly sorry for dragging him into this. "Please, Silas, put him down! He did nothing wrong, let him go."

"Why should I listen to you, woman? This does not concern you. Now run along, and go fix us some lunch, huh?" He pinches my cheek harder than he probably should, and then follows that up by patting my rear end in full sight of the small crowd that has formed on the street. I am mortified. And just about ready to see Silas' corpse on a spit like the fresh game that Pa sometimes brings home. Except there's nothing fresh about this sluggard.

"It does concern me, as it appears that you're both fighting about me, even though there's no need to. In less than two weeks, I will be *all yours,* Silas. So leave Finn alone - there's nothing he can do to change that. There's nothing anyone can do to change that." I place my hands on my hips, and hit him with my best withering glance, not totally unlike the one I used on Ma just a little while ago. He tries to return it, but ultimately falters, throwing Finn to the ground and stomping away in the opposite direction. I kneel down to help him up.

"Finn! Are you all right? I'm so sorry he interrogated you like that. I will never understand why he is the way he is, although I have a sinking feeling I'm about to find out."

Finn accepts my hand and I pull him up the best I can. He rights himself, and then rubs the shoulder that Silas had assaulted. "I'll be okay, Constance. Thanks anyway."

159

Something about him seems a bit more strained than he was even just earlier today, as he could barely look me in the eye. I have no idea what changed, but something definitely did. I guess I'll have to be okay with that, somehow. But I certainly wasn't going to give up without a fight. And the time I had left before I am joined to Silas forever should be spent with the guy I really wanted - and that is most definitely Finn. It's always been Finn, and it always will be.

CHAPTER 18

That was the closest call yet. How in the world am I expected to do this? It seems like I can't go very long at all without being apprehended by some humanoid. Maybe my clothes really are far too eye-catching... The next thing I should try to do is maybe get some more Earthly ones. But where should I get those? Is there a shop somewhere? I believe I should have some Earth currency in here, yes, here it is. Good. Now, to find a shop.

Griffin walks around the main square of the town, hoping that no one will give him a hard time as they have been up until this point. After about half an hour of aimlessly walking around, Griffin finds a nearby cart with what appears to be clothing for sale.

"Hello, do you sell clothing here?"

The woman turns around to face him, and rakes her eyes up and down his unfamiliar frame. "Yes, we do. What may I help you with, kind sir?"

"I would like a full outfit, as would be typical for my gender and species."

The look on her face does little to hide her confusion and concern with her newest customer, but nevertheless, the woman picks up some slacks, a shirt, and jacket that the common Puritan man would wear. "Try these on."

Griffin begins to disrobe right there, but she stops him. "No, not here! There's a partitioned tent right over there." She jabs an aging finger toward a nearby temporary structure in the marketplace.

"Thank you." Griffin tries on the clothes, and they fit perfectly, so he decides to pay the shop owner, and then continue on his quest, hopefully appearing a lot less conspicuous having trading the baby blue rubber suit for a sensible outfit of gray, navy blue, and black. He even buys a small satchel that he tucks his Upperworld suit into, in case he needs it later. Satisfied with his purchases, Griffin continues down the street, comforted by the fact that it is very unlikely that he is being watched at this point.

Now where did Constance go? Perhaps I should call Onyx for help. He dials up Onyx on his communicator, and is immediately received when he hears his very familiar voice on the other end.

"Yes, Griffin? Is something the matter?"

"No, I just, took a bit of a detour to acquire some more Earth-appropriate attire, and in the process of that, I lost my targets. Can you direct me to where Constance is at this present moment?"

Onyx sighs. "I can only see what you see, as you are our connection to that world in that time. But I'll try. If she's any where near you, I'll direct you."

Griffin then waits for Onyx to search his surrounding location. "Ah yes, it appears that Constance is back at her home. You can find her there, but as you've seen, it is critical that you stay out of her sight."

A dull chill runs up Griffin's back. "You saw all that?"

162

Onyx sighs. "I sure did. You've got to step up your game, Griffin. There are no re-do's."

"I know, I'm trying to."

"Try harder."

"I will. Oh, and I'm also sorry if I had upset you earlier about your mother. I will try to more properly monitor my words in the future when speaking to you about this very sensitive topic."

"I appreciate that, Griffin."

✳✳✳

"Luna? Are you there?" Brielle knocks at Luna's door, trying to psych herself up for the news that she knows she must impart, even against Evander's judgement. She hears some light footsteps pad over to the door, and then the click of the unlock button as Luna opens the door for her.

"Hi Brielle." She pauses for a moment, waiting for any obvious signals as to what she might be there for. "Something I can do for you?"

"Well uh, not exactly, no. I just wanted to come by to… talk."

Luna nods, and opens the door wide enough for Brielle to walk through. "Okay. So, talk then."

Brielle settles herself on Luna's couch and nervously crosses her legs. "Talk? Right. Okay."

Luna sits down in front of her on a plush, white-fur covered chair. "You're acting very odd. Is everything okay?"

Brielle notices that Luna's face is subtly stained with old tears, as if the sadness and the fear she must undoubtedly be feeling continues even after the initial crisis. Having never felt sadness or cried herself, she finds it hard to relate to her, but tries to be gentle and thoughtful regardless. "Not completely, and actually, I've been told not to tell you this, but I think I absolutely have to."

"You have to tell me... what exactly?" Her voice lowers, seemingly bracing herself for the blow.

"Onyx is stuck on the throne."

Luna audibly exhales. "Well, yes, I was aware of that. Is that all?"

Brielle shakes her head. "Well, no, not entirely. You see, he's not doing well."

"Well I am aware how hard it must be, and I can only imagine how he's feeling about it because it's killing me being apart from him. But Griffin and Evander are working tirelessly to set him free, and then when they do, everything is going to be okay. So there's no need to worry." Luna smiles at Brielle, and then gets up off the couch. "Would you like something to drink? I'm gonna get some water."

"No, I'm fine, thank you though. And no, that's not the whole story."

"Oh?"

164

Brielle gulps back the concerned lump forming in her throat, but it still hurts less than the guilt and feelings of betrayal digging a pit in her stomach. "So... he's not doing well, as in, the throne and the current it carries, is slowly sapping away his life force, the longer he's on it."

The glass of water hits the floor and shatters, as Luna remains completely silent, frozen in place, in the middle of her pod. "What... what exactly do you mean? Like, the same way Zephyr was weakened? No, no, he can't be... Zephyr was on that throne for eons, since the beginning of time. That's impossible."

Brielle shifts uncomfortably in her seat. "Well, we have to remember that Zephyr was a Titan, appointed eons before time began. He was well-equipped and able to handle it for as long as he did. Onyx, on the other hand, wasn't meant to hold that position for any longer than he really has."

Luna sinks down onto her couch again, barely even acknowledging the broken glass on her floor. "So... what do we do? How long until..."

"We don't know, Luna. I'm so sorry. It's going to take a little time, maybe more than we have. I wish I had better news. Evander made me promise not to tell you, but I couldn't help myself - I felt that you had the right to know. Wish I said something sooner."

Luna remains silent, not even crying yet. Her face appears stone-like, as if waiting out the response would make the painful reality dissipate faster. But it won't, and she refuses to budge. She sits there in complete silence as her insides scream her name, and all the plans, hopes, and dreams that she had for Onyx goes down a receptacle tube into the great unknown.

CHAPTER 19

"Good morning, class!" I force myself to smile as cheerfully as possible to my class, even though it is the beginning of the last week I'll ever be teaching them. This week would be incredibly sad, but it will likely be nothing compared to next week, when I'll be knee-deep in wedding planning, including dress fittings, and who knows what else. I am dreading it, all of it. The end of this week will mark the beginning of my own life phasing out so my own personal death can begin.

"Good morning, Mistress Miller." I smile at the chorus of their voices greeting me, and I make a mental note to store that in my memory, as I will surely miss it. In fact, the list of things that I know I will be missing has been growing steadily longer every day, as my inevitable marriage to the miserable slug grows closer every day.

"I have some unfortunate news to share with you, students. I am so sad to announce that I will be ending my term teaching you all here in this schoolhouse at week's end."

Hushes and whispers float among the gasps in the room. "But Mistress Miller, we love you teaching us here!" Many of the other students nod their heads in approval, and I feel my eyes watering at their outpouring of appreciation toward me. "Yes please, do stay Mistress Miller! We'll be good, right everyone?"

"No, no, it's nothing you've done wrong, absolutely not. Not even you, Johnathan." I nod to the troublemaker in the back row, who shrugs at me even though a small smile threatens to form on his face. "I am actually due to be married in less than two weeks' time, so preparations must be made. I'm ending my stint here at week's end, and Mistress Mary Smith will be your new teacher."

I'm instantly met with a chorus of moans and groans, complaining about how boring Mary was last time she came to substitute teach when I fell ill for a week last year. "Now now, don't speak so harshly of your new school mistress, I am sure that you will learn a lot of wonderful things from her."

"Mistress Miller, who are you betrothed to?"

I swallow uncomfortably, as I realize that I will have to reveal the source of my dread. After all, I have always wanted to be married, but perhaps not this soon and definitely not to Silas, not in a million years. "I will be joined in matrimony to Silas Brewster." I nearly gag as those words escape my mouth, and Fae notices that from across the room, as her eyes widen and she averts her gaze from me as to not call attention to my unfavorable reaction.

"Well, congratulations are in order, Mistress Miller!"

I turn to my left and force a smile on behalf of the very sweet and thoughtful girl next to me, my favorite student. "Thank you, ever so much, Bitty."

"You must be so thrilled!" She claps her hands happily, and I remain stumped as to how to be honest without sullying Silas' reputation. After all, he does that all on his own.

"Well, I can honestly say that it will certainly be a change of pace." I smile politely, and then turn back to my desk before I have to entertain any more comments. "Time to take attendance now, we have much to do today. Emily Alcott?"

"Here."

I continue down the list until every student is accounted for, and then I open my copy of their primer. "We should review your spelling list for the exam on Wednesday. You've all remembered and studied over the weekend, correct?"

Some students excitedly nod, while the vast majority shrug or sheepishly look away. "Now, I know it's not the most exciting thing in the world, but it is quite important, nonetheless. So, let's get to work."

✳✳✳

"Where is she now, Griffin?"

"She's in the schoolhouse with the young humanoids, Onyx. I'm watching her through the window."

"Good, keep an eye on her."

"I will."

Griffin clicks off his communicator, and then watches as the students appear to be leaving the schoolhouse, at least temporarily. They run out of the building excitedly, making a beeline for the school grounds. If it's anything like what they did a few days ago, he expects them to return to their studies shortly - it's only a brief afternoon reprieve to allow them to get their energy out. Griffin decides to walk around the periphery of the grounds to get a better look at Constance, preferably without arousing suspicion. His new clothes are already making that a lot easier than it was before.

Unfortunately, Griffin doesn't consider the fact that even in disguise, a strange man skulking around a schoolyard can also look very, very bad.

"Excuse me, who are you and what is your business here?"

He turns around with a start and finds himself face-to-face with the very reason he's there in the first place. "Oh, uh, hello. I'll just be going, I mean, sorry." He turns to walk away, but the girl grabs his shirtsleeve and doesn't let go.

"Answer my question, or I will have you hauled out of here faster than a horse-drawn carriage chasing a sugar cube vendor."

Her blue eyes pierce his, and he feels a shiver crawl down his spine. He mumbles the first thing that comes to mind: *"You look just like him."*

"What? Who do I look like?" She backs away, visibly unsettled.

"No, sorry, I didn't mean to, I really should be going. My apologies, Miss." Griffin tips his hat as he's seen other male humanoids do, and then makes his way back toward the main path. Constance stands still,

170

watching him walk away. Griffin dares only to turn back once, just long enough to take in her surprised expression and the way her dress flows in the warm afternoon spring air.

"Mistress Miller, who was that?" Constance looks down at one of her students, who also saw the mysterious character on the school grounds.

"I haven't the faintest idea, Bitty. Was he bothering you?"

"No, but he was just standing around watching everyone, and I thought it to be rather odd."

"It was very odd indeed."

"... and that's why I absolutely require it to be done exactly to my specifications. You understand that, right Evander?" Onyx leans back on his throne, his cavernous blue eyes growing darker every moment.

"Absolutely, I understand you completely." Evander lowers his voice a bit, and after looking around the Grand Hall, he asks Onyx the question that has been on his mind. "So how are you feeling?"

Onyx sighs audibly, and shoves his hand angrily through his flaming hair. He shrieks when his hand touches the flames. "You'd think I would have kicked that habit by now."

Evander awaits the answer to his question, so set on it that he doesn't even flinch at Onyx's cheap attempt at humor. "Seriously, I've been worried about you. I mean, everyone is, but especially me because of... what you told me before." Evander motions to the throne, and then back up to Onyx's now almost completely pale face and sunken eyes.

"Well, I don't feel good."

"I figured as much."

"I mean, I'm hanging in there, but it hurts. All of it. I hate feeling stuck more than anything, and I hate that Luna probably needs me and I can't be there for her. Everything about this is even worse than I could have ever imagined."

Evander nods and sighs. "None of us knew that there would be this many repercussions. We may have saved the Upperworld, but we might have lost you."

Onyx looks down at the impeccably-tiled floors and frowns at his reflection. "Sometimes I wonder if the Upperworld was even worth saving."

Evander's jaw drops. "Um, come again?"

Onyx sits up a bit more, as if to punctuate his point with more emphasis. "Well, I mean, I just don't truly see how really necessary it is. I bet humans can make their own decisions. Especially after living around them for a bit, I've seen that they are surprisingly sentient. And the energy will just re-route itself to the humans directly, so lives can still be produced and the human race will continue just fine without us. I think what we do is... relatively redundant."

"You're just saying this because you're understandably stuck and very frustrated about it."

Onyx frowns. "Well, that could be part of it, but it's not the only reason. Far from it, actually. I'm just asking you to think critically - why did we ever think that humanoids needed help making decisions? As we saw in my case, they still do what they want. So, why keep them from what they are going to do anyway? As the Earthlings would say, *give the people what they want.*"

Evander stares at the floor between his feet and sighs. "I understand what you're saying, Onyx, but that's... such a radical perspective. I doubt that anything could really be done about it."

Onyx nods, but leans back in his seat again. "That is true, but overthrowing Zephyr was also a very radical move, and we managed to do that. Why can't we do this?"

Evander pauses. "Do what, exactly?"

Onyx smiles as his hair glows a bit brighter the same way a lightbulb would appear over a character's head in a humanoid cartoon program. "I'm saying, let's hit the kill switch."

✳✳✳

"Luna... Luna! Please tell me you're okay. Say something, anything!" Brielle shakes her gently, in the hopes that she'll stop crying long enough to talk this over. "Ugh maybe Evander was right to keep this from you, it seems you can't handle it."

Luna pauses her sobbing, and sits up long enough to glare at Brielle through her tear-soaked eyes. "What exactly do you mean that Evander was keeping this from me?" The words seep out of her mouth monotonously, as if her brain couldn't be bothered to inflect them at all.

"Well, um, he told me... he told me not to tell you."

"Because he thought I couldn't handle it."

"Well, yes. And honestly, I think he was right."

"Brielle?"

"Yes?"

"Get out." Luna points to the door of her pod with a very decisive finger, and Brielle, shocked at her sudden outburst, readily complies.

"Well, okay. Sorry, Luna. I didn't know how to tell you." She sulks out of the door and Luna slams it behind her. She sits back down on her couch alone, but then she realizes that the real beef she has isn't with Brielle at all. No - the real problem lies with Evander, and she intends to address that sooner versus later. With that realization, she rises from the couch like a phoenix from the ashes, and begins her walk to the Grand Hall where she knows Evander has been spending most of his time, both monitoring Griffin and Constance on Earth, as well as keeping Onyx company. If it weren't for her shifts in the Sorting Room, Luna would be there constantly too, but she doesn't have that luxury.

The purple fog that is usually quite calming assaults her face as a reminder of the Upperworld and the injustice that it embodies. After experiencing the freedom and pleasures of Earth, Luna realizes how much she really has come to hate this place. Having something to compare it to definitely stripped off her rose-colored glasses in a hurry and replaced them with a hazy, dark cloud.

I'm going to give Evander a piece of my mind. He doesn't have to like it, but he's going to figure out in a hurry that I might actually have emotions, but they don't weaken me. Instead, they make me stronger. And I'm not someone that has to be protected - not anymore, anyway.

Her deliberate footfalls continue to lead her straight to the Grand Hall, where she plans to tell Evander exactly how wrong he was about her. Sure, she cried, but if she didn't, then that'd be abnormal. How else did he expect her to react to news that the condition that her lover is stuck in is slowly killing him and there is nothing she can do to stop it? There is no end to the incongruities of those with emotions and those without - they might as well be different languages. And the barrier between them is only growing larger with every passing Earth day.

CHAPTER 21

"I noticed how upset you looked earlier about the announcement. I'm so sorry this is happening to you, Constance."

I force myself to try to smile at my very sweet sister, who is obviously sympathizing with my predicament and feels every bit as helpless as I do. "Thanks, Fae. It's going to be okay, it does still repulse me uncontrollably but I have managed to come to grips with it, mostly." I straighten some loose papers on my desk and gaze longingly out to the empty classroom.

"Oh really? So, what have you been thinking about?"

I smile to myself, and try not to blush. I take one more glance around the classroom to make sure there aren't any stragglers left here after hours within earshot. "Well, Finn, actually."

Fae's eyes widen. "Finn Abbott? Our neighbor?"

I nod gleefully.

"Well, what about him?"

I sigh. Fae was still young, but she is also more clueless than her peers oftentimes. "Well, I'm thinking about how good it was kissing him the other day... over and over again."

"What? But you're betrothed to Silas, what if someone saw you?" Fae's eyes stayed much wider than they needed to be for optimal vision, but clearly her shock was more pressing than her personal sense of appearance at the moment.

"I am painfully aware of that fact, Fae. But I realized, that if our parents have the gall to sign away the rest of my life, then I have the right to take what I want with the time I have left. And right now, I want Finn."

Fae nods slowly. "I guess... that makes sense. But you don't think you'll get caught though?"

I shrug. "Hopefully not. But at this point, I'm desperate enough to risk anything. I have an entire life of Silas to look forward to."

Fae shrugs. "You know, it might not be *that* bad. Maybe you'll even come to love him after a while?"

I throw my head back in a full-bodied laugh. "Yeah and maybe you'll fall in love with that fly buzzing in the corner. I think the odds are about the same."

"Well I'm just trying to help." She turns away and finishes packing up her school books.

"Wait, Fae, I'm sorry. I just... I'm dealing with a lot right now. I appreciate you, really. I'm just... trying to process everything. Surely you understand me."

She nods, but I start to truly hate my short temper once I see tears threatening to fall down her perfectly pink cheek.

"I do understand, Constance. It must be really hard on you, being stuck with someone you don't like. But I guess if it were me, I'd be trying to find the good in Silas instead of just counting down the days until my life is over."

178

She storms out of the room and starts walking home. Mother always expects me to walk with her, so I hurriedly grab my things and jog after her through the schoolhouse door.

"Fae! Fae, please, wait for me!" My lungs burn as I push my legs faster than is typical for me to catch up with my poor little sister who I accidentally hurt. "I - I didn't mean to upset you. I really am sorry, and I appreciate your thoughtfulness."

She stops speed walking just long enough to glare at me, and then resumes her walk at normal speed, but in complete silence.

"Okay, you don't have to talk about it. I don't really want to talk about it either, so that's fine."

We arrive home after a very awkward walk, and somehow the crunching of the pebbles and sand under my feet comforts me.

"Well *hello* there, *beautiful*."

I turn to meet the putrid gaze of my arranged husband-to-be, and have to remind myself not to visibly or audibly grimace. "What do *you* want, Silas?"

He just smirks at me, wiggling his fingers. "You know what I'm thinking about?"

"No, I'm not at all wondering and I couldn't care less."

"Well, you might care about this."

"Look, I've had a very long day. Would you please move aside so I can get into my house?"

He waggles his eyebrows and fingers in unison and then touches my shoulder more seductively than I'd really like. "Not until I tell you what I've been thinking about."

I try to ignore the feeling of his greasy palm soaking through the fabric covering my shoulder and place my other hand on my hip defiantly. "Okay, fine. What is so important that you had to trap me like this?"

He grins wider than a child gazing at a candy cart. "You know what's better than a wedding?"

I shrug. "I don't know, maybe impaling my eyeballs with Mother's darning needles?"

"No, silly, that'd be painful! I mean, *the wedding night.*"

I can feel his eyes try to undress me right then and there, and I'm so disgusted that I push him away and open the door to my house, slamming it behind me. Fae re-opens it to enter.

"Sorry I slammed it in your face, Fae. I didn't mean to."

"Oh, it's okay. And I think I'll recant what I suggested earlier."

"What?"

"About you maybe loving him eventually - I think that might actually be impossible, I'm sorry to say."

I try not to laugh at the delicious irony of it all, but it's easy because the central reason the joke was funny is the very same one I'm convinced I'm going to die inside in a little over a week. "Oh, well, thank you, Fae, I suppose."

She nods solemnly, and I place my sack on its designated hook on the kitchen wall.

"What was all that slamming about?"

Fae and I turn to see Mother entering the kitchen through the backdoor. "Well, we just saw someone we knew and wanted to avoid." Fae smiled sheepishly and I knew Mother was about to pry for more information.

"Well that wasn't very nice, who was it anyway?"

"No one!" I chime in unexpectedly, and Fae shoots me an exasperated glance.

"Interesting. Well, try not to ignore people, in the future please. That's not very neighborly, you know."

We both nod, just grateful to be let off the proverbial hook. "We will, Mother." Our chorus of affirmation tickles her ear in just the right spot, so she grabs he basket of clothes that need mending and goes out the back door into the yard.

"Are we good now, Fae? I really am sorry about all that."

She nods. "We are, and I'm sorry I got so upset at you."

"It's okay, I think I deserved it." I wrap my arms around her, and we stand like that for who knows how long. I'm really going to miss moments like this the most.

Volume Three: The Undoing

CHAPTER 1

"The kill switch? Are you insane? That's not... that would bring about an entire apocalypse. The whole reason you are even on that throne in the first place is to keep that from happening!"

Onyx rolls his eyes, letting the blue light emanating from them momentarily illuminate the cavernous darkness surrounding them in his sunken face. "Yes Evander, I am painfully aware of the implications surrounding the killswitch. The reason I suggested it was because I am at my wit's end, and frankly, I don't really see what the point of any of this is anymore." He waves dismissively at the air around him, likely referencing the entire Upperworld and its theoretical obsoleteness.

"That's a very radical suggestion to make, Onyx. Care to elaborate on that?"

He sighs, and the flames on his head dim slightly as he settles down into his chair. "Well, humans very rarely do as we intend them to anyway. Plus, they should be able to do whatever the heck they want, who are we to decide? The whole thing is quite unnecessary."

"Onyx, this is really unlike you, any particular reason why this sudden change of perspective?"

"Well, I think that even after all my Earth studies, I still didn't quite understand what it is like to live on Earth - that is, until I actually did live on Earth for a short while."

"When you went to rescue Luna."

"Precisely. And since then, I can't stop thinking about how freeing it was, and how I think I was… better off there than I was here."

"You're stuck in a chair here, slowly dying. I don't blame you for feeling that way at the moment."

"But it wasn't just the being stuck in a chair versus not - there is so much more that exists on Earth than it does here. There are emotions, and unions, and desires, and talents, and people of all kinds and backgrounds. I cannot even begin to explain the amount of diversity that is there. Can't you see it? I want to go back."

"Well, you do realize you'd be rendered mortal there - you'd die eventually."

"I'd also die in this chair, what's the difference there?"

"Fair point, but you must realize that I can't just shut down the entire Upperworld on a whim. This would take some careful thought and speaking with the other inhabitants in order to figure out what might be best. Besides, we have Griffin working tirelessly to set you free, so patience is key for that."

Onyx sighs, and looks down at his feet. "I can be patient. But unfortunately, the current waits for no one, and I can feel it beckoning me to the Underworld. I'll hold on as long as I can, but it's getting harder, Evander. It's getting really, really difficult."

"I understand, my friend. But the best thing you can do is to hold on. I'll see about getting you some supplements from the infirmary to sustain you until then."

"That would be marvelous, thank you, Evander."

"Evander!"

Both Onyx and Evander shift their gaze toward the main entrance of the Grand Hall, as Luna storms down the hallway, her face streaked with tears. "You were *supposed* to tell me. I needed to know. *Why did you keep this from me?*"

Onyx and Evander exchange concerned glances, as they realize that their joint attempt to keep Luna from worrying too much about everything going on has epically failed. They appear to be engaged in a staring contest until a raise of Onyx's eyebrow appears to make him victorious. Evander breaks eye contact and gingerly turns to face Luna.

"Well, Onyx told me to keep it from you because unlike me, he has emotions and can feel things that I can't. He reassured me that you wouldn't be able to handle it. And judging by your current state, I'd wager that he was right."

Luna opens her mouth to speak, but seems unable to form words. Rather, she takes a few more steps before crumbling at the foot of Onyx's throne. "I *need* you, Onyx. I need to know how you are, how you're feeling, and what's going on. I'm terrified of losing you and the fact that I may have lost you without even knowing it is making me sick with worry."

"So, you're worried about this, I take it?"

Luna glares at Evander's seemingly insensitive question. "Yes, Evander. With every fiber of my being, I am terrified. And I should have known what was going on."

Evander sighs, and Onyx remains stoically seated on his throne. "I'm sorry, Luna. But I must ask, how did you find out?"

"Brielle was kind enough to tell me - you may not have wanted her to, but I am eternally glad that she did."

"I suppose that makes sense, Luna. I'm sorry I doubted your ability to cope."

Luna shrugs. "I've been through worse, you know."

Evander nods. "I know. And Onyx, though he is silent at the moment for whatever reason, I know he knows that too."

"I do know, that, Luna."

She nods in response, but then has trouble making eye contact with Onyx. It's not because his eyes have grown too bright and blinding, but rather that her fear is taking over her ability to view him as anything besides a goner.

"How long?"

Evander and Onyx exchange glances. "How long what?"

Luna clears her throat and takes a few more hesitant steps closer to Onyx's throne. "How long until his body gives out from the current?"

Onyx looks down at his lap and rests his head in his hands, while Evander suddenly finds the tall ceilings more intriguing than anything else at the moment. "We

186

don't know, but based on how he seems to be doing, it's probably not long at this point."

"We shouldn't have let him on there, I could have done it."

"No, you couldn't have, Luna." Onyx's monotone voice cuts the tension in the room, as both sets of eyes land on him. "You would have survived a fraction of the amount of time that I am, you're a lot weaker than I am, and you have a smaller body mass."

Luna sighs. "Well, if we knew you'd be trapped there, I wouldn't have wanted to let you go."

"Well, it's probably for the best that we didn't know, because it had to be done. There had to be a replacement for Zephyr, you know that."

"I do know that, but I wish it didn't have to be this way."

CHAPTER 2

She's walking to school now, and it seems to be a typical morning, from what I've seen. Griffin thinks quietly to himself as he follows Constance and Fae to school on Tuesday morning. He's being extra cautious about calling attention to himself, as last time, he nearly blew everything, right to Constance's face. But he's had a good night's rest in a nearby haystack, and a decent breakfast on some stolen garden fruit, so he should be able to focus better than ever. If anything, this time spent following Constance has given him a priceless education on how to operate and survive on Earth. The circumstances around which he is gaining it are certainly unfortunate, but the outcome will only be a benefit to him in the future.

"Come on Fae, we're running late again and I have to catch up on some work before the other students arrive!"

He watches as the girl coaxes her younger sister out of their house, and into the bustling early morning streets as the compound begins to wake up for the day.

"I'm coming as fast as I can!" She catches up with Constance and they both resume a more relaxed gait toward the school building on the other side of town.

Darting among bushes and behind buildings, Griffin follows them. He's quickly getting tired of this, though, as the constant following and risk it brings with it is undoubtedly wearing on him mentally. A quick glance to his wearable device displays the current Earth time, and the rapidly flashing digits that reflect the all-important time coordinates. When the key turning point occurs, he knows that he can press the pause button on his wrist to see the coordinates and send them to Evander. Then, and only then, would they agree that he could come back to the Upperworld. And as controlling and stringent that it is, Griffin has to admit that he is starting to miss the controlled and scheduled atmosphere of the Upperworld. The openness and uncertainty of his mission is simultaneously the most daunting and the most exciting part of it.

He settles down near the school building in some bushes, trying not to be visible to anyone in or around it. Fairly satisfied with his spot, he settles in for the time being.

"Hey there, Nobody. Whatcha doing here at school?"

He winces and hesitates to turn to the source of the voice assaulting his ears. "I'm not doing anything. Go away and *stay* away."

The nauseating Earth child settles down in the bushes next to him instead. "Nah, school is starting in a few minutes. So I'll stay right here. You're way more interesting than school anyway." He grins widely, his missing teeth highlighted by the gaping holes in his malicious smile.

"Well, fine. But be quiet."

"Don't be quiet, you say? All right, if you insist."

And then the child begins to scream in the most blood-thirsty manner he could manage, until Constance herself appears from the schoolhouse and runs toward the source of the screaming.

"Calm? Is everything all right?"

"There's a man here, and he was bothering me."

Her face turns red with anger, and she marches right over to where the small, grubby, chubby finger is pointing. "You again? I'm going to have to ask you to leave."

"I'm sorry, I didn't do anything to upset the child. He came over to me."

She perches a hand on her hip. "Well, that may be possible, but why were you sulking in the bushes near a school?"

Griffin has to think of something to say, and fast. "Well, I've been observing you."

"Oh really? Why, exactly?" She crosses her arms, probably equal parts intimidation and protection.

"Because... I wanted to see how you teach without any knowledge of being observed by an outsider."

"And why is that?"

"Because... I would like to teach someday." That isn't a complete lie - Griffin has been considering guide training for a while, which is basically like the Upperworld version of a schoolteacher.

"Oh, I see. Well, that's interesting, considering that most men work in the field. Don't you have a plantation to upkeep or something of that nature?"

"No, I do not."

"Oh, I see. Well, I do know you're watching me now, so how about I let you watch me from inside the schoolhouse? I'll even introduce you to the children."

Griffin hesitates, but then nods slowly. It's not quite the method he was working toward, but upon further thought about it, it might just be crazy enough to work.

"Good! Let's go then." She then turns to the despicable child who had gotten him into this mess in the first place. "Come along, Calm. I expect your completed lesson on your desk before the bell rings."

"Yes, Mistress Miller." She pats him on the back and then walks with Griffin toward the open door of the schoolhouse.

"Class, I would like to introduce a new friend to you who is going to spend the day with us. HIs name is..." She cups her hand around her lips to whisper to Griffin. "What's your name? I don't believe you said it before."

"Griffin." She nods.

"This is Goodman Griffin, and he will be joining our studies today. Anyway, it is time that we return to our times tables."

An echo of moans and groans fills the room.

"Now now, don't be upset. This is important for any profession you might take up in the future. Now, who can tell me what seven multiplied by three is?"

A petite girl with dark-haired braided pigtails raises her hand. "That is twenty-one, Mistress Miller."

"Excellent job, Amelia! Now, what is seven times four? Does anyone remember?"

Griffin fights to stay focused amidst the very dry content that is in front of him - and he marvels at the way most of the children seem to be completely enthralled, excitedly waving their hands in the air to get Constance's attention. She must be a very special teacher indeed.

CHAPTER 3

It was quite strange finding this mysterious man in the bushes - and I am pretty sure he is the same one I saw in the schoolyard the other day, except that his clothes seemed much more sensible this time. Somehow, he persuaded me into letting him watch my lesson with the children. I still am not sure quite why I allowed it, but I did. So now I'm standing at the chalkboard, jotting down vocabulary words while the students spell and define them for me.

"Yes, fabulous job, Hanson. I appreciate your efforts!"

This continues on for perhaps another hour or so, and then I reward the children with a slightly earlier lunch break and an extended outdoor recess. The mysterious stranger follows them outside, which does concern me for a moment, but I relax as soon as I see him settle himself on a nearby bench just outside the door where I can see him. In the snowy season, many times we must stay indoors where it is a bit warmer with the fire in the hearth, but this spring has been such a lovely reprieve from that miserable existence. If only there was a metaphorical spring to rescue me from the eternal winter I was about to enter into with Silas.

"Good day, Mistress Miller."

A much deeper voice than any that my students possess greets me from the open doorway, and I immediately feel my cheeks heat up.

"Hello, Finn." I smile happily, and walk over to him, perhaps a little too quickly. "What are you doing here? It's the middle of the day, after all."

He grins, pulling me closer. His clothes smell of lingering sweat and fresh laundry. His mother makes the most wonderful lavender soap this time of year, and the smell suits him. The floral tones of the aroma float up into my nostrils and down into my mouth, licking my throat in anticipation.

"I just, really wanted to see you. Pa told me to take a break because he had to bring some of his tools to be repaired, and he could probably tell I was getting rather fatigued anyway. So, I took a leisurely walk to see someone... interesting."

"Oh really? And who's... interesting to you, right now?"

His smile grows even wider, and I flinch as I hear the floorboards of the small entryway platform creak under some unexpected weight. The mysterious stranger is looking in on us, and that's when I realize that no matter how pleasant it may seem at the moment, having Finn visit me at school could start some very ugly rumors and complicate things.

"Constance, who's that?" He jabs his thumb in the general direction of the doorway.

"That's, um, no one. Really. I only just learned his name this morning."

"Oh? And what is his name, and his business here?" He starts to walk slowly toward the visitor, and I begin to realize that Finn may be assuming things that are not true.

"Finn, his name is Goodman Griffin, and he's here to observe my teaching. That's all."

"Is that so?" Griffin nods silently, as if to strengthen my claim. I appreciate his effort, but quickly realize that his hesitation to speak about it may call more suspicion onto everything.

"Well, don't you find it a bit odd that a grown man like him doesn't have a field to work in? Where is he even from?"

I shake my head. "He didn't say. Well, I'll ask him." I walk gingerly over to where Goodman Griffin is leaning against the doorway, staring at us both. "So, uh, where exactly are you from?"

His eyes glaze over, as if I asked him to build me a new wagon out of thin air. "Surely you must be from somewhere. Do you just not want to tell me?"

He nods.

"Okay, it seems he's not disclosing where he's from. That's all right, isn't it, Finn?"

Finn's crossed arms and furrowed brow remind me that everything is very likely not at all okay, and that I may have just unwittingly dug myself into a deeper hole than I can reasonably expect to get out of before my marriage next week. So I do the one thing I feel will work to show him how I feel - I lean forward until my lips touch his, and kiss him more passionately than ever before. He responds, and I feel his left hand find my lower back and tug me even closer than ever before. As electricity passes back and forth from my feet to the top of my head, I quickly back away. I momentarily forgot that a student could walk in at any moment, and have more questions than I would feel at liberty to provide answers for.

"Finn, you should go."

"So, was that how you wanted to say goodbye?"

"What? No, I didn't mean an absolute goodbye, I meant, goodbye until after school later." Then I lower my voice even more, to emphasize my point. "They could walk in here at any moment, you know."

He blushes, as he realizes what I mean, and a shy smile passes over his still-pink lips. "Oh, right. I forgot. I guess... you have that effect on me." He winks, nearly imperceptibly, to anyone but me, simply because I'm standing close enough to him to see it.

"I promise I'll come by later, okay? I just need to get through the rest of the school day."

Finn reluctantly nods, and then turns to leave. He awkwardly squeezes past the visitor, and then makes his way to the main road before disappearing amidst the students making their way back to their desks in response to my ringing of the bell.

"Welcome back, class! Did you enjoy your recess?"

"Very much, Mistress Miller."

"I am so glad to hear that! I did too." I tried to hide the blush forming on my cheeks by looking down at my feet, and then the textbook I laid out on my desk to introduce to the children next. "Today, we are going to do some collaborative reading and reciting. Please open your primers to section one, chapter thirteen…"

✳✳✳

"I'm holding on as long as I can, Luna. It'll be okay. I'm going to hold on for you." Onyx's eyes dim slightly in the hazy light of the Grand Hall, and Luna's eyes fill with tears.

"I know that, Onyx. I really do. But I can't help but wonder… if maybe you just won't make it."

His hair flares up in response, but the flames die down as quickly as they began. "You're right, Luna. I can't lie to you. This is risky, but I don't have any other choice. I am stuck here, for better of worse. And it's not like I really have room to regret it, as we absolutely needed a replacement and I am convinced I was the only one who could handle it, at least for as long as I have."

Luna takes a few more steps closer to the throne. "It's killing me, not being able to be close to you."

"I know, I'm feeling so numb, and it's terrible. I'm sorry, Luna. I'm sorry everything had to happen this way. I feel like I failed you."

"No."

"No?"

"You were brave. You did what had to be done. And even though it may come with a price, I can't imagine that the alternative would be any better." She nods respectfully at him, as if to solidify at least an emotional distance from him, perhaps so that their separation wouldn't hurt so much anymore. Letting him go would hurt her more than anything she has experienced before, but the pain is necessary. And from it, Luna will grow into a new being, free from attachment to anyone else and completely autonomous in every way. Luna Alison Nelson is going to let go of Onyx Dalton Miller, even though it very well may be the last thing she ever does for him.

CHAPTER 4

"There's definitely something happening between Constance and Finn, I watched them earlier. It shouldn't be too long now, I would think."

The receiver he wears beeps back its affirmation, and Griffin hears Onyx respond on the other end, many years and dimensions away. "That's good to hear, Griffin. I'm... not doing so well."

"Oh, really? What... what's happening?"

A pause meets him on the other end of the receiver. "I don't want to worry you too much, just status quo. Just hurry, please."

"Will do. I'm making good progress with Constance - it seems that she has invited me into her inner social group."

"What? What do you mean?"

"Well, she sort of found me in the bushes... and she invited me to observe her while she teaches."

"That sounds far too invasive, Griffin. I need you to step away. If you change the past too much, there could be dire consequences."

"Believe me, I know that. But this is better, trust me. Now I don't have to skulk around her so carefully. I have a backstory now."

"A backstory? And what exactly would that be?"

Griffin pauses, to try to convey the information in words and contexts that Onyx would be able to understand. "Well, she's a schoolteacher, as you know.

And I changed my clothes recently to better reflect things that would be worn by people in this millennia, so I appear more of a natural fit in this society. I told her that I don't own any land to farm, so I am studying to be a teacher also - which is the reason I have been skulking around rather menacingly."

"And the reason is what, exactly?"

"The reason was that I was observing her habits to learn how to be a teacher as well."

"And she believed you?"

"Appears so."

"Oh. Well, I suppose that's fine then. But you must understand that the closer you get to her, the greater the risk of tampering with the space and time narrative. Is that clear?"

"Crystal clear."

Griffin clicks off his transmitter and walks back toward the schoolhouse, hoping to reconnect with Constance before she leaves for the day. He reenters the doorway, where she and her sister are talking quietly amongst themselves.

"Hello again, Goodman Griffin. I'm just packing up for the day. You're free to go."

Griffin realizes that since she is aware of him now, he can't just follow her unnoticed. He quickly thinks of a reason to stay near her. "Well, I'm actually fairly new around here, would you mind if I accompanied you back to town?"

Constance exchanges a glance with her sister, and then shrugs. "Well, I suppose that's all right. I do have someplace to be though, so I'll take you to the center, and then you'll be on your own from there, okay?"

Griffin nods politely, and even tips his hat before letting Constance and her sister lead the way out the door. He's picked up a lot of subtle humanoid habits just by osmosis alone.

"So this main road leads through this area, and goes straight into town. And that, over there, is the Edwardson's farm. Fae used to love playing with the baby sheep there in the springtime, it was so funny -"

"Did not!" Fae pipes in, seemingly to defend her status and prestige.

"But you did! Perhaps not too recently... had to have been at least a year ago."

"Nah, those are just for babies."

"*Sure* they are. Anyway, moving on…"

The conversation continues like this for the rest of their walk, and Griffin nods enthusiastically, even though he has become quite familiar with this surrounding area, as of late. Before he knows it, he finds himself back in the center of town.

"… And that's about it! School resumes tomorrow at eight o'clock sharp, so will I see you then?"

"Yes, that sounds good. Thank you again for your help."

"Don't mention it. God be with ye." Constance is about to walk away, she locks eyes with the terrible Silas as soon as she turns.

"Well lookey-lookey, who is my lovey traveling with today? I hope he isn't your boy toy - that would be quite disrespectful, you know."

His rotten breath and puckered, scarred skin assaults both my nose and eyes. "No Silas, Goodman Griffin here is a new coming schoolteacher who has come to observe my class. I was merely showing him back to town. Now let me go."

Griffin's face turns white, as he remembers what Onyx said about avoiding messing with anything that would change the overall narrative. "Constance, I should really be going now. See you tomorrow." He leaves the two squabbling humanoids where they stand in the town center, and does his best to vanish as quickly into the crowd as possible, while still viewing his target from a safer distance. What he doesn't see, is the brown-haired boy with the shaggy head of hair staring him down from a nearby alleyway with his arms crossed and a red face. That's phase one of a potentially changed narrative.

Griffin sees him just a bit too late, and his own face becomes visibly pale as he watches him walk directly over to Constance's house, to meet her at the front door. The conversation they are about to have likely won't be a pleasant one, but necessary, all the same.

CHAPTER 5

"Constance, I saw you walking home with him."

"What? With who?"

Fae rapidly excuses herself, once she sees that the conversation I'm about to have with Finn might not be something I want her to hear. "I'll go do my homework, see you later, Constance."

"That... random person you were with. What's his business with you?"

"Finn, just let me explain, I think you're getting upset over nothing!"

"Oh nothing? Now, whatever is going on between us... is nothing?" He lowers his voice, which I appreciate, as well as the way he conscientiously leads me away from my front door so that my parents wouldn't be in earshot.

"It's not nothing - but the Goodman Griffin is. He's studying to be a schoolteacher and observed my class today. He's new in town and wanted to be walked back to the center marketplace. That's all."

"Oh."

I can hear the air dissipate from his lungs and the tension loosening in his chest. "Precisely. I wouldn't hurt you, Finn. I know this..." I motion in between us, as there really is no accurate word to sufficiently describe what is really going on. I settle myself on a nearby barrel, and run my hand over the rough, weather-hewn wood and continue my thought. "... I realize this is unconventional, to say the least. But you knew that, and you understood that it was temporary because of... my situation."

Finn nods, his face more relaxed but his hands still showing signs of stress - wringing them like a damp rag is never a good sign, I know that much.

"I understand, Constance. I'm not sure why I jumped at it like that, I should have just asked you first."

"Perhaps. But I'm sorry I upset you, I'll try to be more sensitive about that. It's hard, balancing everything. My life is about to change forever and there's nothing I can do about it. It's terrifying, and daunting to process. Surely that makes sense, right?"

"Of course. I can only imagine what that must be like."

"And for your sake, I hope you never find out."

He smiles sweetly at me, in that way that makes me absolutely weak in the knees, and then he pulls me closer in a tight embrace, breathing softly near my ear and planting a chaste kiss on my cheek. "Let's take a walk, maybe? Do you have some time for that?"

"I can make time, let's go." I look around to make sure no one is around, and I grab his hand. We both walk toward the woods and green spaces that have yet to be turned into farmland or plots for new houses as a part of the expansion that has been happening around town as of late. With both the rapid population growth and the visitors who never leave, we are running out of space.

"I just got very uneasy seeing you with him at school today. I was shocked, and didn't know what to expect, you know?"

I nod, and give his hand a reassuring squeeze. "That makes sense. And even though I'm engaged to someone else, we have an... understanding for now, right?"

"I like that... an understanding. That makes sense, I think that covers it."

"And you're okay with... letting go eventually?"

Finn's eyes suddenly glaze over, and I'm worried I upset him again. "No, I'm not. But I'm going to have to be."

I exhale, and stop walking long enough to give him a big hug. His touch fills me with a hunger that I didn't know I had, and suddenly he's kissing me again, more desperately than ever. I can feel all the longing, and the pain that he feels. His lips tell a greater story than words ever can.

✳✳✳

"I think I messed up, Onyx."

"What do you mean, *you messed up*?" Griffin can hear the intensity growing in his voice, and prepares himself to take whatever Onyx is about to dish out.

"I made your father upset with your mother."

"How?"

"It's not important, what's important is, I have to fix that. Can you have Evander locate Constance's approximate location in relation to me? I had eyes on her, but I had to walk further away from her."

"I'm on it. Evander, please find her for Griffin." He hears some discussion in the background through Onyx's receiver, and waits for further instruction.

"Okay, she appears to be in the woods not too far away from your current location. Find her immediately, but don't let her see you this time!"

"Copy that."

✳✳✳

His hands find their way to my waist, tugging desperately at my apron, and I practically tear it off. My head covering falls to the grass in an unceremonious heap, and I let my hair fall loosely among my shoulders. Before I know it, we're both kneeling in the lush, green grass, and then lying down together. He's easing himself over me, and I quickly realize where this is leading. I don't want to make him stop, but I feel like I need to.

"Finn... Finn..."

"Mmhmmm?"

He continues kissing me, sucking my breath away, but I finally manage to come back to the surface.

"I can't do this right now."

"Huh? Oh, okay." He brushes off his pants and sits back in the grass, rubbing his eyes with the palm of his hands. "I didn't mean to pressure you."

"You didn't, don't worry. I just want to think about it first."

"Of course."

I remember to grab my head covering and apron from the grassy forest floor where we dropped them, carefully brushing them off the best I can. And then I hear some rustling in the nearby trees. "Finn, did you hear that? Is someone there?"

He looks up from straightening up his own clothes, and alarm registers on his face. "You don't think it's -"

"No! I mean, I'm not sure. I hope not... let's go!"

Finn grabs my hand to help me up, and then we both take off at a feverish gallop back toward the main path and the town. If Silas catches us in the throes of passion, I have no idea what would become of me, and I certainly do not want to find out.

CHAPTER 6

"Did he find her okay?" Evander approaches Onyx's throne, and he nods slightly. He's become very weak at this point, and so he's been conserving his energy to be able to survive as long as he can.

"Yes, I believe he did. Based on the live footage we have of Griffin, I think he just got a bit too close to where she was, and they heard him coming. But overall, I think things are going as planned, aside from a few *close calls.*"

Evander sighs, and shifts his weight to lean against a nearby marble column that reaches from the impeccably clean tiles to the cavernous ceiling of the Grand Hall.

"Where's Luna? Could you... check on her for me?"

Evander shrugs. "I could, but I doubt she's very happy with me at the moment. Perhaps Brielle would be a better choice? I think I should give her some space right now."

Onyx nods, and then signals for him to ask Brielle to check on her. As Evander leaves the Grand Hall to get Brielle for that very purpose, Onyx's flaming hair dims the darkest it's ever been, and he lays back limply in his seat. They are rapidly running out of time - and no one knows how long it will be before Onyx succumbs to the current, just the way Zephyr did.

✳✳✳

In response to Evander's suggestion that someone check on Luna, Brielle knocks on the door to her pod. "Luna, how are you doing? Evander suggested that I check on you." Brielle waits there for her momentarily, expecting the door to open revealing a tear-stained and very upset Luna. But what she sees when the door unlocks surprises her.

"Oh, hello Brielle! Come on in. What can I do for you?"

"For me? But I came to check on *you*."

"Check on me about what exactly?"

Brielle's eyes nearly pop out of her head in bewilderment. "Onyx? Don't you miss him?"

Luna inhales deeply before any tears can fall, steadying herself against potentially debilitating emotions. "Yes, of course. But I'm trying not to."

"Why? It's understandable, if you do. I mean, I don't understand, since I don't have the ability to experience emotions, but for you, in your case, it's logical, I suppose. And now I'm babbling, because I always babble when I'm nervous and I never know how to calm down until someone tells me to calm down and-"

"Brielle! Calm. Down."

"Oh. Right." She nods erratically and then sits on the nearest chair next to the front door of Luna's pod.

"I have come to the conclusion that there is a very slim chance that Onyx will both survive this and be able to be with me the way he used to, so I'm letting him go."

"What do you mean? Onyx still needs you. If you give up, then he'll have no reason to stay alive."

Luna shakes her head slowly, and tosses her long, dark hair over her shoulder. "I'm not the only reason - he also has to stay alive for the sake of the Upperworld. That's a good enough reason to press on, that's for sure. Besides, we're all doomed anyway when he eventually passes, so there's really no reason to fight it anymore. I'm choosing to go down as calmly as possible."

Brielle's jaw drops open, and she stands up slowly. "Luna, were you medicated somehow to feel like this? Please tell me they didn't do this to you..."

"No, I don't think so. I'm fairly certain, anyway. Just believe me when I say, he's not worth worrying about anymore. He is as good as gone. In fact, I feel nothing at all."

Brielle takes a closer step to Luna, and looks directly into her eyes. They're glazed over, but still very purple. "I don't know, Luna. You don't look so good."

Luna places a hand on her hip. "What? I feel better than ever. What do you think is wrong? I can assure you, I'm totally *fine.*"

Brielle catches the wrist that Luna waved in front of her, and takes a good look at her implanted device. "Luna, does your device usually glow orange like this?" She drops Luna's wrist so that Luna herself can take a good look at it.

"I'm not sure, but I did have a new one implanted, as my original one was expelled on Earth."

Brielle's eyes widen as she puts the pieces together. "Luna, they *are* drugging you, remotely, through your device!"

"What? That's impossible! I didn't request any kind of medication. Why would they do that?"

Brielle grabs her hand. "I truly have no idea, but I have a feeling we're about to find out. Come on!"

"Where are we going?"

"The medical offices, they'll know what's going on."

Luna nods. "You seem pretty concerned, is this a bad thing?"

"Of course! If you didn't ask for it, they are changing your personality and natural predispositions against your will. We need to fix this immediately."

"Oh, I didn't even think of that!" Luna starts to panic, subconsciously scratching at her wrist to make the unwanted effects go away.

"You can't fix it yourself, you know. We have to get you looked at. I'm so glad I questioned it, Evander was concerned about you too."

"Did he know about this?"

"No, none of us did. I just found out, remember?"

Luna nods. "Oh, right. Why did I forget that?"

Brielle's face goes pale. "Oh my pod, it's affecting your short-term memory too. This is bad, Luna. I don't think this is just any kind of "feel good" cocktail they put in your system - I think they're trying to control you."

"What? Who again?"

Brielle sighs. "Just come with me, I'm going to get this sorted out right away."

CHAPTER 7

"I saw both targets in the grass all alone, and I was so sure it was going to happen, but it didn't. I have a feeling it will be soon though. How is Onyx doing?"

Evander sighs on the other end of the receiver. "Well, not well, but that's not exactly news, I suppose. Just keep on doing what you're doing, Griffin. All your efforts are greatly appreciated."

"And Luna?"

"What about her?"

"How is she holding up?"

"Well, she's been acting a bit odd, actually. I sent Brielle to check on her. Everything is coming relatively unglued up here, we're looking forward to getting you back soon."

"Me too, this Earth stuff is pretty bizarre. I think I'm much better suited for the Upperworld."

"Well, I'm not so sure that's a good thing. The way things are going, you may want to get comfortable there."

"What? Why?"

"Well, we're not sure how long Onyx will hold up, and if we can't figure out some kind of a solution, then we may have to relocate everyone down to Earth."

"Really?"

"This is very confidential, but there has been talk of the kill switch."

"*The* kill switch? The one that the Titans installed as a last-ditch effort to save the human race if the Upperworld malfunctions beyond repair?"

"That's the one. But I don't want you to worry too much. In the event of that occurring, we would make appropriate arrangements to get everyone assimilated in no time. The Undercover Earth Guides will all be notified to help with that."

Griffin looks up at the blue Earth sky, trying to process everything that Evander is telling him. "So, how likely is that going to happen?"

"I'd say it's more than likely - in fact, that's probably going to be the default unless we can figure something else out. Onyx wants that to happen - even he seems to believe that our work here is inconsequential."

"What? But that can't be! The Titans wouldn't have appointed us for the work otherwise, right?"

"It's hard to say. Just keep eyes on her at all times - you don't want to miss it."

"Will do, over and out." He ends the call on the receiver and then continues following the couple back onto the main street.

✳✳✳

"Well, uh, thanks for taking a walk with me. I guess I'll see you around." Finn smiles at me, and I feel my whole body heat up. Or perhaps that was a lingering sensation from our time in the field, in addition to the rapid escape from whoever or whatever was watching us.

214

"Thanks for asking me to go for a walk. I'll be around as well. God be with ye."

Finn nods at me, and then starts back toward his own house next door. I watch him as he leaves, and I notice the calm, relaxed way he walks and not-so-subtly enjoy the way the late afternoon breeze ruffles his hair. That boy might just be the death of me, and suddenly, I think I'd be okay with that.

"Constance, where were you? I needed help with my mathematics homework, but I couldn't find you anywhere."

My blushing must have given away my answer faster than I could open my mouth, because Fae's eyes widen and she lowers her voice before dragging me into our shared bedroom. She takes a quick glance around our small house before closing the door and sitting down on her bed. Patting the space directly next to her, she motions for me to sit down and talk.

"There's not much to say - Finn invited me to go for a walk, that's it. I just got back."

Fae purses her lips. "I would believe you... if your apron wasn't on backwards."

I immediately look down and realize that I may have just given myself away.

"And your head covering is a lot more wrinkled than Ma would like, I'm sure. What exactly were you up to?"

I sigh. "Nothing really."

"Really?"

"Well, okay, I suppose I've been caught. It was…
leaning in that direction, but I stopped it."

"You stopped it?"

I nod slowly, trying to find the appropriate words
to explain this to my twelve-year-old sister. I knew that
she had been made privy to the ins-and-outs of what I was
toying with recently, and she had yet to become
comfortable with the idea as a whole. "But next time, I
might not."

"Well of course not, you'd be married, you'd have
to-"

"Oh, not with Silas, goodness no. I meant… with
Finn." I lower my voice to barely above a whisper, as I am
terrified of the possibility that Ma or Pa might hear what
I've been thinking about.

"Oh."

"Indeed."

"Do you really think that's a good idea?"

I shrug. "Well, I don't think that being forced to
marry someone I absolutely despise is a good idea, so why
does this have to be? I've decided that I am taking back
my life, at least for the next week and a half, or so. And I
don't want my first time to be awful."

"It might not be."

Her voice shrinks in stature considerably, as I can
see that the morals that she had been taught by our ever-
so-mighty parents has left her feeling very conflicted, and
rightfully so - I was breaking all the rules they had tried to
instill in us since we could walk. Infidelity was one of the

worst things we had been warned against, and I know that being betrothed to someone was as good as being married in some compounds. It varies quite a bit by family, and ours is undoubtedly on the more stringent end of that spectrum, but I'm not about to back down on what I know I needed to do. I only have one beautiful, wild life, after all. And I refuse to spend the rest of it pleasuring that miserable slug. At least for now, I might be able to go down into that awful existence with a good memory or two to get me through.

"Silas doesn't care about me at all, Fae. So of course it would be awful. I need something good for myself, surely you see that?"

Fae looks down at her lap, and very subtly, shakes her head. "I don't know, Constance. I don't think I can completely understand you. This just seems wrong to me. But I promise not to tell Ma or Pa - I wouldn't do that to you."

I frown, but exhale with relief. "Thank you, Fae. I appreciate that. And I don't expect you to understand, but I really do wish you would."

I get up to leave our room, and close the door behind me. I don't know exactly when it's going to happen, but I'm so glad that I have someone special like Finn who loves me to share it with.

CHAPTER 8

Arriving at the infirmary, Brielle and Luna ask the receptionist at the front desk to be seen immediately by the doctor who replaced Luna's implant.

"Well, I can see what his availability is. I think he might be booked solid for the next few shifts…"

Brielle speaks into her own implanted device. "Evander, I need you to send a required examination notice to the infirmary right away, with Onyx's authority signifying it. Thank you." She remains staring stoically at the receptionist, who receives a notification only mere moments later.

"Ah, it seems something's opened up. Have a seat, I'll let you know when the doctor is ready."

Brielle makes a face at the receptionist and then proudly leads Luna to one of the seats in the waiting room. "Just gotta learn how to leverage your resources - and lucky for you, we're tightly knit with the head of all things in the Upperworld."

"Evander?"

"No, Onyx, silly."

"Who?"

Brielle's eyes widen, and her blood runs cold. "What do you mean, 'who'?"

"I mean, I'm not sure who that is."

"Luna, I swear, this is not the time to be joking…"

"I'm not joking, Brielle, I honestly have no idea-"

"Hello! I'm Doctor Amaranthus. Oh, Luna, is everything all right? What can I do for you today?"

Brielle glares at him with the energy of a thousand lasers. "No Doctor, everything is absolutely not all right. She can't remember who Onyx is."

"Onyx? The stand-in for Zephyr, right?"

Brielle nods. "They were sort of destined to be together, you see. And then with the whole altercation about him taking the throne, things have been difficult and he wasn't doing well. Luna has been having some trouble processing it, and then just as soon as she started to absolutely break down, she just... became really numb, and then forgot. Granted, I can't relate because I'm not half-humanoid, so I can't feel emotions, but typically she can and I find it concerning that she suddenly can't feel anything *and* forgot who her destiny was."

The doctor nods, completely devoid of any kind of reaction.

"Why are you not reacting to this? Can you fix it?"

"Well, I only fix problems. This isn't an issue. Her embedded device is doing exactly what it needs to do - isn't that nifty? One of the new upgraded features includes a self-dispensing calming medication, specially medicated for half-humanoids like Luna, actually. Unfortunately, a small side-effect of it includes some loss of short and long term memories, but it's worth it to be spared of those pesky emotions, don't you think?"

Brielle's jaw drops, and Luna just remains sitting next to her, lacking any visible reaction.

"No, I do not think that is good at all! Please disable that feature, please."

"Unfortunately, there's nothing I can do about it once the panic has triggered the release. But this really is for the best - now she can focus on sorting, which is very important work."

"But she won't even need to sort pretty soon! The entire Upperworld is going to be obsolete, don't you understand? None of this matters anymore! But what does matter..." Brielle grabs a nearby decoration off the wall, and takes the sharp end of the metallic, abstract art and presses it to the doctor's jugular. "...is that my friend here can go back to being exactly who she is without you randomly changing her personality with medication she never asked for! Do you understand me?"

The doctor doesn't even flinch, but instead raises his wrist to his lips and calls for backup. "Security, please." The words croak out of his throat with a significant amount of labor, and he has to struggle to breath, as his back has been quite literally pressed up against a wall with Brielle holding the sharp end of some abstract wall art to his throat.

"Just disable the device, and I can let you go away unscathed. Because if you don't, I am *fully* prepared to jab this through your neck, and never look back."

"Step away from the doctor!"

The security agents aim a stun gun at Brielle, who begrudgingly agrees to back away.

"Now leave him alone, and take the patient with you. You are both no longer welcome here."

"What? But she needs medical assistance!"

"You should have thought of that before assaulting a medical professional. Now leave before I decide to use this on you for real this time."

Brielle grabs Luna's hand and pulls her out of the infirmary. "This is for the best, Luna. They're useless, anyway. I'm sure Evander will be able to help you."

"Help me what?"

"Oh boy. I better get you some help quick! You don't sound so good."

"What?"

"Oh Luna, this is so upsetting! Who told you to get that implant? Did you even really need it?"

Luna's eyes clear for a moment, and she comes back to the surface. "Uhmmm I think it was Vidia? She thought I should have a new one installed."

"Well, she thought wrong. I'm about to exchange some words with her, actually."

"What?"

"I'm going to take you back to your pod to rest, and then we'll figure out a solution. Try not to worry."

"Oh, I'm not really worried at all. I feel... just fine, actually."

"And that is exactly what worries me."

CHAPTER 9

"I just took her to her pod. She was acting odd because the new device that she had implanted drugged her."

"What? Are you sure?" Evander's eyes are wide open, shocked at what Brielle has reported.

"The doctor just reported that directly to me. And now, Vidia is going to have some explaining to do."

"Oh my pod…" Evander rubs his eyes with the palms of his hands, and tries to process the news that he's hearing. It's not the first time things have happened outside of his control - far from it, actually. But he's getting weary and worn, and this is just the icing on the cake. As if worrying about Onyx wasn't enough, now Luna might also be ruined forever.

"Okay, well don't tell Onyx."

"I will be telling Onyx, Evander. Because last time we tried to keep information from those two, things ended *so well*."

Evander sighs. "You're right, Brielle. I'm sorry to keep putting you between them like that. Do what you think ought to be done."

"Thank you, I will."

The two stand in silence for a moment, in a small hallway in the Grand Hall, wondering about what is going to happen next. For eons, the Upperworld ran perfectly, without any issues like this. But that all changed the day that Luna materialized.

"I should go talk to Vidia -"

"Okay, if you're sure. I'll go try to remove the implant and then let Onyx know what's been going on."

"I am. Check back with me after."

Evander nods, and then Brielle heads to the Sorting Room, where she is relatively certain that Vidia will be on her shift. After a short walk on the main pathway and through the security gates, Brielle sees Vidia's fuchsia colored hair toward the right.

"Vidia. A word please."

The fuchsia hair turns around rapidly, and Vidia's mouth forms a small 'o'. "Certainly! Just a moment please." She very unceremoniously drops an orb into a receptacle tube and them pats her hands dry on her pants. "What can I do for you?"

"I need to know why you drugged Luna." Brielle barely lowers her voice, or even tries to monitor her wording. At this point, she doesn't even care, if she ever really did.

"What? I absolutely didn't do that. But can you keep your voice down? People are staring, you know." Vidia's cheeks begin to match her hair, but Brielle isn't even remotely sorry. She taps her toe in a rhythmic pattern on the sorting room floor, and her crossed arms seem to be shielding her from any more lies.

"Oh, but you *did*."

"No, I didn't. I wouldn't have any reason to do that to Luna."

The eyes of the sorters around them follow the conversation like a tennis match, moving back and forth, waiting for the return volley.

"Well then explain to me why she suddenly lost the ability to feel emotions or remember things about Onyx since she panicked and apparently triggered an automatic medication to be administered?"

The small 'o' her lips made before grows into a full-bodied horror as the color also drains from her cheeks, rendering Vidia more like a ghost seeking asylum on this side of the realm rather than a sorter who made a grave mistake.

"I didn't know that would happen... is that a new thing that they made?"

"Some kind of upgrade, is what I heard."

"Oh my pod, Brielle, I had no idea. I should go apologize to Luna."

Brielle's curt hand gesture stopped her in her tracks. "Don't even bother - we're in damage control now. Perhaps if Evander removes it, things will return to normal."

Vidia slowly nods. "Oh, all right. Well anyway, I think I might take my break now. There's no way I can focus after all this. Again, I really am sorry."

"Sorry doesn't fix this, but I'm sure Luna would appreciate your apology nonetheless."

✳✳✳

"Luna? Can you open up? It's Evander."

"Who?"

"Oh my... please, Luna. I can help you."

Luna opens the door to her pod, and as soon as she does, recognition returns to her face. "Oh, Evander. Okay. I've just been a little... slow on the uptake lately. I'm not totally sure why, really. Probably just overtired."

Evander shakes his head. "It's a bit more than that, actually. I'm sorry to say this, Luna, but I'm going to need to remove your implant."

"What? Why? I just had it installed recently - my wrist hasn't even fully healed yet."

Evander nods sadly. "I know, believe me I do. But the problem is, the medication its dispensing to you is robbing you of your personality. I need to remove it so you can feel again. It's also making you forget things. Please, Luna? I know it's scary, and I'm not exactly a medical doctor, but I should be able to reopen the wound and slip it right out. Can you let me do that? Please?"

Luna's eyes narrow, and she shakes her head. "I can't let you do that, Evander. It will hurt too much. Besides, every sorter needs an implanted device. It's so I can be notified at any time from anywhere in the Upperworld or beyond."

It's like she's been brainwashed. Well, good thing I brought this cloth doused in nitrous oxide. "I'm sorry Luna, but this is because I care about you, and I know Onyx does too."

Evander swiftly covers her mouth and nose with the cloth, and after only a few seconds and a mild struggle, her eyes flutter shut, and he lays her gently on her couch. Throwing the cloth on the floor, he grabs some sterile equipment that he pilfered from the infirmary, and begins to work on reopening the wound and removing the device.

CHAPTER 10

The remaining school days of this week both dragged by and moved far too quickly for my liking. I know it's my last week on the job, and I am determined to soak in every moment of my life before chores and a husband become my ultimate focus. At least I was able to help Goodman Griffin by allowing him to observe me - I felt so very flattered that he found my classroom to be effective enough to want to emulate it when he himself begins teaching. And he has proven to be quite helpful, what with the chores, and even monitoring the children during their recess and break times. But there's also just been so much on my mind surrounding my unwanted betrothal and my very-wanted relationship with Finn, even if it has been short-lived. I know Mother and Father would be horrified if they found out what my plans were, but I rationalize that I was equally horrified when I found out their plans for me, so right now, this just feels like delicious payback for the horrid life they have resigned me to. But Fae promised not to say anything to them, and even though she didn't approve, she did promise, and I trust her.

"Well class, as sad as I am to say this has been our last day together, I want you to know that I have so loved teaching your class. I wish you all the best, and I truly hope that you continue to enjoy your education throughout your remaining years of study. Your new teacher will be joining you on Monday. Have an enjoyable weekend, and may God be with ye." I am immediately met with a chorus of children saying their condolences and that they will miss me, which truly warms my heart. I had no idea my time teaching would be ending too soon, but this moment will be one that I will store away in the corners of my mind to help me through the tough times that are undoubtedly coming for me.

The students give me many hugs and sad smiles, and then file out the schoolhouse door. I watch them leave for the last time, and then gather up the last of my belongings. "Fae, where are you? It's time to get home."

"I'm coming, Constance!"

I turn around to see Fae running toward me from the field, carrying a very crude but sweet bouquet of flowers. "I picked these for you, Constance. I will surely miss you being my teacher."

Suddenly, tears begin pricking the corners of my eyes - and I told myself I wouldn't cry, at least in front of any students. But Fae is also my little sister, so I allowed myself to have a good cry with her, which was surprisingly calming.

"Thank you, Fae, this was so very sweet. I will miss this too." I clean myself up, and then we both head out the schoolhouse door. We resume our typical chatting as we walk home, but then turn around to see Goodman Griffin walking behind us at a respectable distance.

"Constance, does he always follow us this way?"

I nod my head. "I'm fairly certain he lives nearby where we do, so it only makes sense that he follow us home."

"Oh, okay."

We arrive home at the typical time we always do, and then Fae settles down in the kitchen to do her homework.

"You know Fae, I can still help you with your homework from time to time, if you ever need it."

"I know, thanks, Constance."

I nod, and then announce that I'll be taking a walk. I open the door to leave, and find myself face-to-face with my beloved - not my betrothed.

"Hey, Constance. Care to take a walk?"

I smile broadly, and tell myself that I'm totally happy with however this goes. "Where to?"

Finn shrugs, and I notice the way that his auburn-brown hair perfectly eclipses the sun. "I dunno. I'll think of something."

I nod, and follow him, grabbing his hand. We both decide to take the back pathway, away from the main road, to decrease our chances of Silas seeing us.

"So Constance, I didn't mean to pressure you the other day. I hope you don't think badly of me, I won't try that again."

I shake my head. "You don't need to apologize, because you didn't. And besides, after taking some time to think about it... I actually really want to."

Finn raises an eyebrow. "You do?"

"I'd like my first time to be with someone I love, and not someone I'd like to see meet an untimely death."

He blushes immediately, and I realize what I just admitted, so I feel my cheeks heat up too.

"You... you love me?"

I nod excitedly. "I really do, Finn. I'd happily marry you if I could."

He looks down at the ground, and then I see a single tear fall down his face. "Constance, you have no idea how badly I want that too." He sighs.

"But obviously, it seems that's not meant to be." I smile sadly. "But it can be, at least for now. We can pretend... I'd like to forget about my terrible future, as well."

We walk along in silence for a bit, and I recognize the cliff that we went to the very first day when we spent time together and I kissed him. I feel his hand wrap around my waist, and I sigh at how nice that feels. Then I turn to look at him, and smile at his face and the way his eyes sparkle in the mid-afternoon light. I feel our lips draw close together, and then they touch in an explosive frenzy. I wait for the spark to fade, but it doesn't. It grows stronger with every passing breath. And that's when I decide that the time is now... and I don't ask him to stop. I give myself over to the desire I've kept under wraps for a while now. Years, actually. I don't hesitate, not even for a moment. And the happiness bubbling up inside of me compensates for the slight guilt gnawing at the back of my mind, but I push it aside, rationalizing that I'll never be allowed to be this happy ever again, so I decide to embrace it.

***

"Onyx, I have the coordinates. Tell Evander to try these ones..." Griffin rattles off the set of numbers that are listed on his wearable wrist communicator.

Onyx's voice immediately brightens at the prospect of finally getting off the throne that has imprisoned him for what has felt like ages. "Thank you, Griffin. I'll pass that along. It's worth a try. But keep in mind, that my conception was likely not the defining moment - rather, it was the moment that she decided... to abort me." His voice falters at that realization, and Griffin notices that he falls relatively silent for a few moments.

"Onyx? Are you all right?"

"Yes, I'm okay, Griffin. This is just... quite uncomfortable for me to talk about."

"I completely understand."

Onyx clicks off his communicator, and tells Evander the coordinates that Griffin provided. After waiting a very uncertain amount of time, Evander returns to the Grand Hall, and a subtle shake of his head tells Onyx what he had guessed - that his conception was not the defining moment at all. Onyx nods his thanks anyway, and Evander looks down at his feet in embarrassment.

"It *was* just a theory, you know. I can't guarantee that the correct coordinates will even work to move the current from you to a more remote configuration. But I figured it was worth a shot."

"I couldn't agree more, Evander, and I thank you for trying."

"Oh and Onyx… you should know something."

Onyx tiredly raises his eyebrows, and awaits Evander's explanation. "Yes?"

"So Luna's new implant… had an unfortunate upgrade… which medicated her into losing her emotions and some of her memories. As the infirmary was completely useless in accommodating our request to have it removed, I had to operate on her myself."

"You did? Is she… okay now?"

"Still sleeping from the nitrous oxide when I left her, but Brielle, Vidia or I will check on her very soon. I wanted to keep you updated on her current state."

Onyx sighs, but nods his thanks. "I truly appreciate that, Evander. Thank you for keeping me informed." He slumps back on his throne, looking worse than ever.

"Onyx, you don't look so good, I'm going to request some nutrients from the orderlies to keep you strong. Hang in there, buddy. We are almost there."

CHAPTER 11

"Constance…"

I wake up next to Finn on the soft grass of the cliffside. We must have fallen asleep, and now the night sky greets us as I come back to the surface. He had the decency to drape my dress over me as soon as he woke up, so I wouldn't be left exposed to the elements or any prying eyes.

"Finn, it's late! I have to get home." I try to get up, but my dress-turned blanket falls off of me and I shriek.

"You may want to get dressed first."

"I know, I just didn't realize how much time passed. Well, don't stare at me!"

Finn laughs, and turns away. "You're just… really beautiful, Constance."

I pause for a second, and smile to myself. "You're all right yourself, Finn."

I finish dressing myself, and tell him he can turn around again. "Finn, my family is probably worried sick by now, I need to get home!"

"Okay, okay, I'll take you home."

"No! I mean, I don't think they'd be too pleased to see you under the circumstances. How about you walk me back to the main path, and then I'll go the rest of the way alone?"

"But it's late, will you be all right?"

"I'll be fine. But let's go."

He grabs my hand and smiles at me the whole way. I knew this was the right choice, after all, now I have another happy memory to store with all the others. And that's the most important thing, I decide. It's all about taking my life back, and this is a step in that direction for sure.

I arrive home and realize that my hunch was right - my family is pacing very angrily in the kitchen.

"Constance! Where were you? What has gotten into you? We were so concerned..." My mother wraps her arms around me in a tearful frenzy, while my father stands in a calm distaste in the corner of the room, like a bad omen.

"I went for a walk with a friend and lost track of time, I'm very sorry I worried you." I straighten the head covering that I remembered to replace this time, in hopes that my facade is believable.

"Do you realize that being out without anyone knowing where you are does not bode very well for a young woman currently betrothed?"

I nod my head solemnly, but even I can't completely quench the fire growing in the pit of my stomach.

✳✳✳

"Luna? Are you doing better now?" Vidia lets herself into Luna's apartment after Evander gave her the access code to make checking on her that much easier.

"I'm doing okay, Vidia. My wrist hurts, but I'm okay."

"Well of course it does, you've been operated on with minimal anesthetic."

"I was what?"

"Oh my pod, you didn't know? Evander removed the device that I practically forced you to get. I came to apologize."

"Well thank you, but I didn't want him to."

"What? But you've got your emotions back! I mean, I assume you did, since you seem pretty angry right now. I'm actually not sure if I should be happy about that or not at the moment."

"Vidia, it was so much easier not to feel anything at all. Onyx being stuck, it was so much better when I didn't love him as much as I do or even remember him. Now everything is just flooding back, and it's hard to handle. I wanted to be able to exist without the pain, don't you see it?"

She purses her lips, trying to absorb what Luna is explaining to her. "I understand that, but it's who you are, for better or worse. You wouldn't be the same without your emotions and your feeling for Onyx. Even though I can't relate to that, I can tell it was important. You were practically a zombie without them."

"But you and all the rest of them don't have emotions, and yet you seem fine. Why?"

"It's probably because we've never known anything different. But you, Luna, were always meant for a bigger and deeper existence than any of us could ever dream of. Embrace that."

Luna slowly nods, and then reclines back down on the couch where Evander left her.

"Would you like to go see Onyx? I'm sure he's worried about you, especially since Evander told him about what happened with your implant and everything."

"Oh, okay, I suppose. I guess the pain is just something I'll have to deal with."

"Well, we can probably get you some medicine for your wrist…"

"I meant the emotional pain, Vidia."

"Oh, right."

Vidia accompanies Luna to the Grand Hall, nodding politely to the other sorters and record keepers that they pass by. "He's going to be happy to see that you're okay, you know."

"I know. I just really wish I could touch him again, and let him hold me again. I miss that."

"Uh, okay. Well, hopefully things will work out and you'll be able to soon. You know, without being vaporized upon contact."

Luna glares at Vidia for that comment.

"Too soon? Okay, duly noted. Sorry."

CHAPTER 12

"Onyx... ONYX! Stay with me here. Come on, you've got to stay strong. If you won't do it for yourself, do it for Luna."

The sound of her name reverberating on the Grand Hall snaps Onyx back to the surface. Very weakened at this point, he subsists only on the name of his beloved and the nutrients that are being pumped into his system, thanks to Evander's request to the infirmary.

"I know, Evander. I'm doing the very best I can. I just hope it's good enough."

Evander smiles sadly. "That's just the thing with you, Onyx. Your best is always good enough, because it's you."

"What do you mean? Everything is going wrong. I'm probably never going to get off of this pod-forsaken thing, and Luna will be left without me. Not to mention the entire human race..."

"No, stop. Onyx, you cannot do this to yourself. Remain calm, and stay strong. There is nothing more you need to do except try to stay alive. Do that for Luna, at least. If you let go of your own accord... there's no coming back from that for her. She'd be absolutely ruined. I'm convinced there is a future for you both, and I'd really like it if you were around to see it."

Onyx sighs, and mumbles some kind of explicit Earth-jargon which Evander doesn't recognize the exact meaning of, but can assume what is meant from its harsh consonant sounds and the exasperated context it is used in.

"We're doing everything we can for you, just hang in there, buddy. Just hang in there. Please."

✳✳✳

The next few days, which I was expecting to be some of the saddest I'd ever experience, were actually some of the best I've ever had. Throughout the beginning of the wedding planning to a despicable boy that I am still convinced I would hate forever, I feel surprisingly calm. Maybe it was the lingering feeling of Finn's lips on mine, or our blissful night on the hillside together, but I am so deliriously happy thinking about Finn, that I think my parents are actually thinking I've warmed up to the whole betrothal arrangement. They couldn't be more wrong, but I suppose it is for the best that they aren't on my case about it anyway.

That was until my blood didn't come when it was supposed to. It's never really happened before, so I usually don't worry too much. But now... well, there could be *something*. I'm not sure what, but the knot in my throat and the pit in my stomach collides with the guilt of what I may have just done, and I feel myself nearly collapse on the washroom floor.

This can't be happening. Maybe it's nothing, but it could be something.

I sit on the floor, and draw my knees up to my chest. I must be taking a while, because Ma raps politely on the door.

"Constance, are you doing all right in there? It is almost time for your fitting."

I roll my ears and try to swallow the terrified tears slipping down my throat. "Yes, Ma, I'll be right out." Washing my face can't fix everything of course, but at the moment, I'd hate for Ma or anyone else to find out I was crying. They'd ask why, and I wouldn't have an answer, since I wouldn't really know. I'd have my suspicions, but that's not something I feel at liberty to even share.

I try to swallow the little voice in the back of my head, telling me what I decide can't possibly be true - that I'm with child, and it's Finn's. Of course it's Finn's, it'd be impossible to be anyone else's. But that's not happening, it can't be. I'm due to be married in less than a week - to someone else. I wash my face as well as I can and tell myself not to worry too much, since I don't have any definitive answers as of yet. That is, until I open the door to my very impatient mother, and promptly projectile vomit all over her. She's less than enthused, and I am mortified and terrified all at once.

"Constance! What is the meaning of this? How disgusting! Now I have to go change. Go meet with Goody Evelyn in the kitchen for your fitting. You have better manners than that, I am astounded!"

My face turns pale, and I mumble some hasty apologies to my mother, who thankfully is too distracted with her soiled garments than the possible reasoning behind it all. And that's the moment I know the truth - that I *am* with child, there's just no getting around it.

I begrudgingly meet Goody in the kitchen, and put up with being stuck with pins and various other sewing contraptions as my mother's dress is tailored to fit my more slender frame.

"You look positively beautiful, Constance." She smiles at me sweetly, and I manage to nod politely at the older woman.

"Thank you very much, Goody." I try to return her hug, but I immediately produce what was left of my stomach contents over her shoulder.

"Oh my, Constance!"

"I am so sorry, Goody. I'm not feeling very well today." And that's my first mistake, as I realize only moments later.

"Not feeling well - I can see that! We must get you to the doctor immediately - can't have you ill for your wedding later this week!"

"No, no, I don't think there's a need really."

"Nonsense! Hopestill, are you aware that the bride-to-be seems quite ill?"

My mother appears in the kitchen wearing a different dress, completely devoid of my half-digested lunch that I so brazenly deposited on it only minutes before. "I had my suspicions, after I had to change my clothes. Did she become ill on you as well?" Mother motions to the fluids and bits of food that I deposited over poor Goody's shoulder as well.

"Indeed. Get this girl to the doctor immediately."

Mother nods, and places a strong hand on my shoulder. Now I know that I am as good as done for, and I'm terrified to find out what happens next.

✳✳✳

"Evander, tell Onyx I'm getting really close to the moment now. This might just do it, stay tuned."

"That is wonderful news, Griffin. Thank you for the update." Evander walks closer to where Onyx is seated, and yells loudly to get his attention.

"Onyx! I wanted to tell you that Griffin is getting really close to the time coordinates we need. We are almost there."

Onyx nods almost imperceptibly, and then resumes his dejected posture. "Thank you for letting me know, but I refuse to get my hopes up. I'll celebrate if I get off this thing."

"*When* you get off this thing."

"Sure. Whatever."

CHAPTER 13

The doctor examines me thoroughly with his very cold instruments, poking and prodding me quite harshly, while my mother looks on with daggers where her eyes should be. I can't shake the feeling she can read my guilty conscience right through my head covering - I wouldn't be surprised, really. After ages of waiting for him to stop his very thorough and invasive examination, he sighs, and tells my mother what I had been assuming as of late.

I'll never forget the look on her face - the amount of blood my body didn't shed like it was supposed to seems to ironically drain from her face.

"I'm sorry, Goody Miller. This is unprecedented, to say the least. And quite shocking - isn't she set to be married to Silas Brewster at week's end?"

My mother's voice seethes with the heat of a thousand bonfires. "Yes, she most certainly is."

The doctor shakes his head disappointedly, and then glances around to make sure we are alone. He leans closer to me, his rank breath hitting my nose almost as sharply as his tools practically mangled the most sacred parts of me. "You know, you don't have to tell him *when* it was conceived, you could just wait a few days. After your wedding, you would have been likely to conceive right away anyway."

My throat chokes up with the guilt of what I must admit in front of both my mother and the family doctor.

After a very pregnant pause, I force the three words out of my mouth, barely above a whisper.

"It's not his."

My mother immediately faints from the shock of my confession, and as the doctor immediately reaches down to help her up and bring her back to consciousness, I take the opportunity to run away. I'm not sure where, but I just had to get out of there. My mother was suffocating me in the moment I needed her most, and that doctor just revealed my worst secret and defiled me in front of my own mother. It's at this moment that I am grateful beyond high hope that my father was not present for any of this, as he would likely have insisted upon coming to the doctor with us, and I think I would have rather met an untimely death than go through that. I run out of the doctor's abode, not-so-demurely straightening my dress to cover my previously exposed rear end. Without any other idea, I run straight to the marketplace in tears, praying that Rafaela might be there to console me. The older girl has become more of a mentor and mother to me than my own mother is, and if I ever needed her, now would be the time. I don't think I've ever seen her in the marketplace on a Wednesday before, but I reason that perhaps I never get to come at this time, as I'm usually in school, had it not been for my stepping down from my teaching position.

"Rafaela! Hello!" I run over to her cart, waving my arms erratically. Her previously relaxed lips round themselves into an "o", and her bright, purplish eyes sparkle with excitement, probably from seeing me at a different time and day than usual.

"Constance! It is lovely to see you unexpectedly, what a lovely surprise! Is there something I can do for you?"

I sigh, and practically fling myself into her arms. "Well, you see, I'm not sure there's much anyone can do." For the first time since I figured out what's been happening with me, I let myself have a good, long cry.

Rafaela gently holds me close, rubbing my back, even though I haven't been able to tell her what the matter is yet. As soon as I cry all the tears out of my eyes, she pulls back from the hug and smiles at me sweetly. "Do you think you'd be comfortable telling me what's got you so upset now?"

I nod slowly. "Well, you remember Finn, right?"

She nods. "Oh, my darling, did he break your heart?"

I shake my head. "No, absolutely not. I actually love him more than ever."

"Oh, and you're still betrothed to Silas."

I nod. "That's not the worst part though."

"No?" Her long, dark hair flows delicately over her dainty shoulders. "Well, what could be worse than not being able to marry the man you love?" She pauses for a moment, and I cringe as I watch the recognition fill her face. "Oh my... Constance, when I encouraged you to enjoy life before the wedding, this is not what I had in mind."

I nod, starting to tear up again. "It wasn't what I had in mind, either."

"Does anyone know yet?"

I shake my head. "Just Ma and the doctor."

Rafaela sighs. "Well, people will know very quickly, news travels fast. And it's not going to bode well for you when they find out..."

I shudder, thinking of all the punishments infidelity would incur. Being betrothed was as good as married in many compounds, including ours. "Rafaela, I'm so scared."

She nods. "Well, I'd say... go tell Finn. Talk to him."

"That's it? That's all you're going to say?" My tears blur my face, and I try to keep myself from screaming at her, because she's hugging me again and clearly feels very sorry for me.

"Well, there *is* one more thing that I could perhaps suggest..."

"Yes? Please, anything, I'm desperate."

She sighs, and reaches down to a very secret compartment of her cart. Reaching down to a little drawer with a secure latch, she produces a small, glass vial filled with a cloudy greenish-yellow liquid. "This is only a *last* resort, Constance. And I truly hope you don't have to use it. But if you do, the herbal pulp mixed in here will terminate the child, and it will be expelled from your body. It's not something I would suggest, as it is far from ideal and it will be very painful, but if you absolutely need to, in order to preserve your own good name and have a good life, swallow this entire vial in one go. That would do the job."

She looks down at the ground, probably ashamed at what she had offered me. But I am so grateful to have a way out of this mess - at least, part of it, anyway. "Thank you so much, Rafaela. What do I owe you for it?"

She shakes her head profusely. "Absolutely nothing, Constance. I'm just doing what I can to help a friend. I will be thinking of you."

I nod, and give her one more hug before tucking the vial into my secure apron pocket where I usually deposit the eggs from our chickens.

CHAPTER 14

"Evander! Why is he not responding to me?" Luna looks over at Evander who was reclined on one of the plush chairs in the Grand Hall.

"Well Luna, I don't want to scare you, but he really is dying. We're working as fast as we can, Griffin said he's getting really close."

"He's not going to die, Evander."

He sighs in response to her desperate plea. "Well Luna, if we can't get him off of that chair with the coordinates that Griffin brings us, I just don't see how -"

"If that doesn't work, then hit the kill switch."

"What? Luna, surely you don't mean that."

She walks closer to him, suddenly much stronger and deliberate than she's ever been. "I am as serious as this whole situation is - and that much is not lost on me, not in the slightest. I refuse to exist without him, so if the coordinates don't work, I will hit the kill switch myself."

Evander's face turns pale. "Now Luna, I know that I don't experience emotions the way you do, but surely there has got to be another way around this."

She shakes her head. "Out of courtesy for you all, I am waiting for those coordinates. If they don't work, I am hitting the kill switch myself. It will stop the current once and for all, and he will be freed. Don't you see that?"

Evander sighs. "I suppose there's not much I can do to sway you at this point. But I would like to know - how did you even know about any of this?"

Luna shrugs. "I've heard you guys talking about it, and I've had a lot of time to think and plan. So the way I see it, you can either help me, or fight me. And given how determined I am, I don't suggest you fight me because you *will lose.*"

Evander swallows a chuckle before it manages to escape his throat. "Well, that's good to know, Luna. I'm not sure about the parameters of everything yet, but I can assure you that I wouldn't dare fight you."

She nods curtly, her long, dark ponytail bobbing ironically happily in the heat of the moment and the tension that is palpable in the room. "Good."

✳✳✳

"I'm following Constance now - she ran away toward the marketplace, and now seems to be running back toward the residential area. I'll keep you posted, should be any minute now, by my estimation."

"That's good to hear, Griffin, as we are rapidly running out of time. Onyx is hanging on by a thread."

✳✳✳

I run straight to Finn's house from Rafaela's cart, and I try to formulate the right words to say to fix everything. I'm not sure what I'm walking into, but I knock on the front door of his house anyway. But before the door can be opened, I react to a tapping on my shoulder behind me.

"Hey, hey you!"

I sigh to myself and roll my eyes. "What do you want, Calm? And why aren't you in school?"

"Ma kept me home because I faked sick real good this time. Isn't that great?"

I smirk a little, but respectably shake my head. "No, Calm, you shouldn't have lied to your mom. You should really go home now and tell her what happened. I'd take you myself but I have some... matters to attend to."

"Whatcha doin' at the Abbott house? Borrowing some butter?"

"Sure, I suppose." I know I just told him not to lie, but I'm not about to explain all this to a ten-year-old, and especially not this one in particular.

"I don't wanna! It's so fun to not be in school."

I nod, but gently nudge him toward his own front door across the way. "Just trust me on this, you'll appreciate it later."

"But I don't wanna!"

I open my mouth again to speak, but I'm interrupted by a familiar voice behind me. I turn to see Finn's gorgeous, sparkling eyes behind me.

"Constance? What are you doing here?" My face pales again, and I nod toward the annoying ten-year-old throwing a tantrum in the middle of the street in the most inopportune time possible.

"Well, I've got to talk to you."

Finn smiles and leans against the doorway. "Okay, well then, talk."

"No, not here. And besides, Calm is… definitely not… calm at the moment."

Finn rolls his eyes and then steps between me and the wild child. "Go on home now, Calm. Don't make me tell your mother that you've been bothering me today."

"You wouldn't!"

"Oh, but I would. Run along now!"

Calm sighs, and then turns back to his home, defeated. I'm both impressed and relieved.

Finn smiles at me, but then notices my distraught face and motions toward the yard. "I think the woodshed is empty right about now, since Pa's out buying supplies. Come on."

I follow his footsteps, and try to formulate the right words in my head. Nothing that sounds good enough comes to me, so I tell myself to just say it. Easier said than done, of course. My shaking hands and frightened face is about to give me away anyway. We both enter the shed, and Finn closes the door behind us. I turn around to face him, but I meet his lips instead. I wouldn't complain too much, but there's just too much on my mind for me to fully appreciate the moment, so I don't.

"Finn… I have to tell you something."

"Oh, right. Okay, what is it?"

I slowly move his hand to my midsection, and even though there's nothing different to feel there yet, I search his face for recognition.

"Constance, what are you doing?"

I guess I just have to say it, then. "It's yours."

"What is?"

"The baby."

"What? How? No... no." He drops to his knees, and then starts crying angrily. "I can't... I can't be a father... and you're betrothed... and Constance, this is..."

"Scary, I know."

"What are you gonna do?"

"Me? I came here, to talk to you!"

"Okay, okay. I gotta focus. And you're *sure* it's mine?"

"Finn!"

"Okay, okay, sorry. I didn't mean, I'm sorry, it's just..."

I nod. He's reacting better than I did, at least he's able to speak in between the sobbing.

"I just felt like you ought to know about it."

"Well, I appreciate that, but I don't know what you're going to do. Constance, I'm worried about you." He lowers his voice a bit more. "You *do know* what they do to girls in situations like this, right?"

I slowly nod. I've seen plenty of girls tortured or worse in the public eye, made a complete example of in front of everyone. And then it hits me.

"I can't stay here, can I?"

Finn sighs. "Well, where are you going to go?"

And then it hits me like a wall of bricks. "Run away with me."

"What? No, Constance, that's crazy, I can't just…"

"You can't just… what?"

Finn kicks at some dirt under his feet. "I can't just… raise a child. Constance, I can't be a father, not yet. I'm not ready."

"Well? We'll figure it out together. I know where my parents keep the money, I'll take a whole bunch. We'll grab everything and run away now. Maybe you can take one of the horses while your pa is in town, and -"

"No, Constance, I can't be a father right now. I wouldn't be able to provide for a baby, there's absolutely no way."

"Well I can't stay here! If I do they'll probably torture me or something. Please Finn, you have to help me! Besides, I know I've been trying to process everything but… I can't marry Silas. I would rather die."

The permanence of my words and the desperation of my tone isn't lost on him, I can see it register in his eyes.

After a long sigh, he nods. "Constance, if you can get rid of… *that,* I'll run away with you."

I feel my breath catch in my throat, and I remember the vial. Even though it goes against everything I believe in, I don't even hesitate to raise the vial to my lips. The taste of the motley liquid is sweet at first, and then bitter. He questions me as soon as it's done, but I simply nod my head and grab his hand.

"Let's go!"

CHAPTER 15

"Evander, I've got it. Try these coordinates, please."

"Thank you, Griffin. I'm on it."

Evander immediately runs to the system controls, and inputs the time coordinates that are supposed to set Onyx free. When nothing happens, his breath catches in his throat, and he knows it's time to initiate the dreaded plan B.

"Griffin, the coordinates didn't work. I thank you for your efforts, but I'm going to bring you back to the Grand Hall now. Prepare yourself for that." Evander presses the correct button on his wearable device linked to the time machine, and has Griffin beamed back up to the Upperworld and in the present time.

Within seconds, Griffin materializes in the time machine. Evander lets him out, and he rubs his eyes, trying to process what it must feel like to have time-traveled twice.

"I'm back?"

"Yes, you made it. But I can't say the same thing for Onyx if we don't hurry." Evander gestures toward where Onyx is on his throne, the current almost completely sapping his energy from him.

"Wait, is this it? What's happening?" Luna's strained voice fills the void, and both Evander and Griffin look over at her with concern in their eyes.

"We do have to start the process, Luna. We have no other choice." Evander pauses momentarily to look over at Griffin, and he motions toward the entrance to the Grand Hall. "Griffin, make an announcement to the sorters and other workers. We need to also notify the Undercover Earth Guides, as soon as possible. We are shutting this down."

"But… how will humans survive without us?"

Evander pauses. "They're resilient, you know. They'll be just fine. This whole crazy scheme isn't worth losing Onyx over. I couldn't live with myself if something happened… and I know Luna would agree."

Luna nods wholeheartedly, and Griffin pats her on the shoulder. "Okay, let's do this."

As carefully as possible, and without overlooking anything important, announcements are made over the loudspeakers, via Evander taking charge of the operation.

"Attention all Upperworld beings, we are hitting the kill switch, I repeat, are hitting the kill switch. Form an orderly line toward the transport room, so that we can conduct a mass exodus to Earth. Once there, you will be assigned an Undercover Earth Guide to help you assimilate. Onyx has held on as long as he possibly could but his body is quickly giving out. Do not panic, just follow instructions as you've been given. Thank you for your service and your time in the Upperworld. That's all."

Ironically, panic *does* ensue, even though Evander specifically warned them all against it. Regardless, they somehow make it to the transport room in one piece.

"Evander, I'll go hit the kill switch. As soon as I do, I'll need some help lifting Onyx off of the throne - can you get some infirmary personnel to bring a stretcher? And tell Luna that he's going to be okay!"

"I'm on it! Then bring him to the transport room so he can be zapped to Earth. And instruct the personnel to stay with him there, he's going to be very weak. Hurry!"

With fast footfalls, Griffin runs to the main system control room, and carefully launches the emergency switch into the "off" position, permanently. Ignoring the red, screaming sirens that are initiated, he then looks out over the deserted sorting room one last time, and then runs to the Grand Hall to help Onyx off the throne.

"I'm gonna need some help here!"

The infirmary workers rush to his aid, amidst the blaring sirens and the sort of organized panic that ensues. Griffin eases himself up to the throne, no longer worried about being eviscerated, as the current no longer flows through him. "I'm here for you, Onyx. You're free now."

Onyx only manages to mumble a few nearly inaudible words, and then the nurses carefully lift him onto a stretcher.

"We're going to Earth now, just hang tight. Can we get some ambrosia for him? He's fading fast and needs help."

As Onyx receives some nutrients and aid that he needs, the group of workers and Griffin move toward the transport room for the mass evacuation. As the sirens continue to blare, the large, cavernous portal to the

Underworld opens up directly in the middle of the Grand Hall.

"Is that the one that Jade fell into?" Griffin catches up with Evander, Luna, and Brielle, and nods.

"The very same one. And this time, we're going to allow it to swallow everything in this realm. It's time to go to Earth."

After everyone is present and accounted for, Evander takes to the intercom for the last time, as Luna tightly grasps Onyx's tired, aching body on the stretcher.

"It's time, everyone. Please remain calm as I initiate the transport to Earth." Evander hesitates for a moment, looking out over at what remains of the Upperworld, and cringes to himself as the cavernous portal to the Underworld rapidly grows in size and power, swallowing everything into it. And then, as he presses the button, darkness is all there is.

Descending into the nothingness leaves them all at a loss. But it's how it was always meant to be, after all.

EPILOGUE
Five Years Later

"… and the very brave, very strong guide helped her, through everything. They never truly understood why they were stuck in that terrible place in the first place. But they realized, that without it, they never would have met. And meeting, even through the pain and the trouble that it caused, made everything worth it."

Luna continues stroking the pale, blonde wispy hair of her daughter's forehead, leaving a small kiss where her fingers once were.

"Tell me again, Momma!" She smiles up at her raven-haired mother, who had been through so much, and yet remained so relaxed and happy, even while reminiscing.

"Jaci, you know it's almost time for bed. You don't want to stay up all night hearing the same story over and over again - besides, you have school tomorrow!"

The little girl pouts, crossing her arms over her petite frame, and hoping for more of the story that she had come to love. Batting her long lashes framing her bright, violet eyes, she waits expectantly for her mother to cave. Little does she know, that very story is the story of her own origin, and the origins of those who came before her. And those that came before her, fought tirelessly through time and space in order that her own existence would come to be, exactly how it was always supposed to.

"What's all this about?" Onyx appears in the doorway of the pale pink room, smiling at his little family.

Luna rolls her eyes but smiles. "*Your* daughter refuses to go to sleep even though she has school tomorrow. It seems she insists on hearing a story again."

Onyx shrugs, and then plops down on the bed next to Luna at Jaci's feet. "Well, then tell her, I suppose. It's an important story, probably worth hearing more than once."

Luna sighs. "I'll tell her more tomorrow. It'll be hard enough getting her out of bed in the morning." She ruffles her tight, perfect, blonde curls, and gives her another kiss on the cheek.

"What can I say? She loves looking at the moon." Onyx reaches over, allowing his lips to meet Luna's. Their daughter protests, but neither of them care - they're much too in love to care about any of that. The moon and the stars twinkle in perfect harmony as the nuclear family looks on, marveling at the sights and wonders of the things they had seen and experienced, and the way that they had found such a home on Earth, despite the long journeys and struggles they've had. And in the moonlight, the three of them look out the big, wide, bay window of their house at the Boston harbor below, realizing that where you come from, often has nothing to do with where you end up.

THE END.

Thank you so much for coming along on the ride with Luna, Onyx, and all the other Upperworld beings that we've met along the way! As sad as it is to say goodbye, I truly hope that this conclusion is one that satisfies what I assume must be very lofty expectations for the characters you've come to know and love.

Keep an eye out for Luna, Onyx, and Jaci if you live around the Boston area – I'm sure they'd appreciate a local to show them around!

ANGELINA SINGER is a college student studying English, Music, and of course, Creative Writing. In her spare time she enjoys crocheting, and mentoring younger music students at a local music store where she has been studying guitar for nearly a decade. She views her writing as a way to simultaneously escape from and embrace reality, especially through the twisted labyrinth of a dystopian setting as seen in *The Upperworld Series*.

Facebook: @AngelinaSingerAuthor
Instagram: @angelinasingerauthor
Blog: angelinasingerauthor.wordpress.com
Amazon: https://www.amazon.com/Angelina-Singer/e/B0743ZF23N/ref=dp_byline_cont_book_1

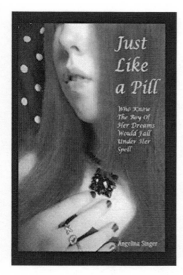

If you liked what you've seen, please leave a review on Amazon and Goodreads!

https://www.amazon.com/gp/product/B07B7MS621?pf_rd_p=d1f45e03-8b73-4c9a-9beb-4819111bef9a&pf_rd_r=W5B8MJ8MXG47BY1W39W4

https://www.goodreads.com/author/show/15565898.Angelina_Singer

BOOK 1: THE SORTING ROOM
BOOK 2: THE FALL OF ZEPHYR
BOOK 3: THE RISE OF ONYX

Made in the USA
Columbia, SC
18 October 2018